D. M. Thomas was born in Cornwall in 1935. His most recent publications include his *Selected Poems* and translations of Pushkin. He is the author of *The White Hotel*, which was an international bestseller and short-listed for the Booker Prize in 1981. His other novels include *The Flute Player*, *Birthstone*, and 'The Russian Quartet', comprising *Ararat*, *Swallow*, *Sphinx* and *Summit*.

D. M. Thomas
SUMMIT

SPHERE BOOKS LTD

Published by the Penguin Group
27 Wrights Lane, London w8 5TZ, England
Viking Penguin Inc., 40 West 23rd Street, New York, New York 10010, USA
Penguin Books Australia Ltd, Ringwood, Victoria, Australia
Penguin Books Canada Ltd, 2801 John Street, Markham, Ontario, Canada L3R 1B4
Penguin Books (NZ) Ltd, 182–190 Wairau Road, Auckland 10, New Zealand

Penguin Books Ltd, Registered Offices: Harmondsworth, Middlesex, England

First published in Great Britain in hardback by Victor Gollancz Ltd 1987
Published in Abacus by Sphere Books Ltd 1988

Made and printed in Great Britain by
Richard Clay Ltd, Bungay, Suffolk

· AUTHOR'S NOTE ·

Summit, an adult fairy-tale, concludes *The Russian Quartet*. The preceding novels are *Ararat* (1983), *Swallow* (1984) and *Sphinx* (1986). The Quartet is dedicated to Alexander Pushkin.

I have followed an ancient tradition in which a serious trilogy is succeeded by a farcical or satirical coda. *Summit* therefore stands on its own, requiring from the reader no familiarity with the preceding novels.

D.M.T.

Nadia was flying home to Leningrad. Drowsy, she was dreaming that Alexander Pushkin was beside her, they were in a troika heading for the sacred early Christian city of Kitezh. The poet was trying successfully to seduce her.

In her lap rested a novel called *Swallow*. She had bought it out of curiosity, simply because its author had once visited her old apartment on the Neva's banks. She had browsed through it vaguely, not liking what she read. Perhaps at another time she might have been amused by a crazy interview being given by an aged, slow-witted American President to a visiting Soviet poet; but this was much too serious a moment in her life. She had closed the book with relief, then closed her eyes . . .

Her dreaming was broken violently by the Aeroflot's sudden nose dive, sending her body, and everyone else's, hurtling forward. Her face crashed into a seatback. Screams, pandemonium, broke out. The nose dive continued, as did the screaming. But Nadia felt calm. She remembered, curiously, what she had said to a British journalist: 'If I awake from death to the sound of Mozart, I shall know everything is okay.'

· I ·

My fellow Americans! A few nights ago I had the privilege
of coming into your homes and sharing with you some of
my problems. I hoped what I told you would have settled
it, but unfortunately there are people around who are only
interested in stirring up as much trouble as possible, so as to
prevent us from carrying out our duties of defending and
serving this great country of ours. I am referring, of course,
to that private tape-recording, made in my office, which
somehow or other made its way on to cable TV and into the
newspapers. And I can understand how many of you have
been upset by the—colourful language which I and members
of my inner cabinet indulged in. Now I make no excuses for
some of the bad language you heard, not least coming from
my lips. I'm sorry; it's not a normal occurrence, I can assure
you; but I would simply point out to you that the situation
was very fraught, we were all a little emotional, I guess, at
some of the unfounded accusations that were being levelled

at the Presidency. All this at a time when many vital issues demand to be dealt with, around the world. Let me spell out some of them to you. The situation in Lebanon. The continuing uncertainty over the health of Comrade Brezhenko. The state of the free world economy. We ought to have been discussing those things, but instead we were having to turn our minds to some—idiotic interview conducted by a drunken Soviet journalist, Comrade Jerkov. Well, if our language at times was a little blue, I think you can appreciate the reason.

And that was also the reason why I said some unkind things, which don't at all reflect how I think of her, about Irma Fleming, that grand old lady of the golden era of Hollywood. I'm a terrific fan of Irma's; Wanda could tell you, if she was here, that I dropped everything a couple of weeks back to watch her when she guested in *Dynasty*. And, boy oh boy didn't she just liven it up! She's a great actress and a great lady. I can understand how my foolish, unintended remarks offended her, and that's why she came out with those couple of letters it seems I wrote her, way back in the days when we were in the movies. I'd forgotten I ever wrote to her. They're affectionate letters, but just the kind of letter an actor would send to his leading lady. As Katie said to me, 'Dad, I get three or four letters a day from actors, and they all start My Darling Katie! It doesn't mean a thing!' And just to set the record straight, I'd like to tell you that when I mentioned wanting to stroke her hot little pussy, which some people have chosen to blow up out of all proportion, I was referring to Irma's kitten. She had, I remember, a fluffy little white kitten, which used to curl up warm and snug on my lap when I'd take a break from the set occasionally and go round to her place on Beverly Hills for a cup of coffee. I fell for that little kitten. Wanda will tell you I've always been a cat-lover; we have three, right here in the White House.

If Miss Fleming insists we had an affair, I can only say I don't remember it! And I don't suppose any man would forget having an affair with Irma Fleming! Irma was always a very romantic lady. I wouldn't like to be discourteous to her. I'll say no more than that she was always a great romantic; she lived her romantic roles to the full and always had a vivid imagination.

I had a long talk with Prime Minister Thatcher over the phone yesterday, and I can tell you she was very understanding about the remark about her made towards the end of our discussion; she understands how these things can get said, just as a relief from tension, after a crisis meeting. Pope Jean-Paul had a very friendly meeting with Vice-President Shrub. A lot of the anti-American demonstrations we've been seeing from Europe were by peace groups heavily infiltrated by the Communists.

I'm glad we've had this further talk. And now I hope we can get on with the business of government. God bless you all, and God bless America!

'That was very fine, sir.'

Henry Requiem, short, thin and neat, fixed the President with a warm smile.

'How do you think it went, Henry?'

'Like I said, I think you did a fine job.'

Walter Mako, his athletic frame bursting out of a tight three-piece suit, murmured gloomily, 'I just hope the Fleming woman hasn't got any more letters up her sleeve.'

'I think we put paid to the Fleming bitch.'

'You're damn right, Mr President,' confirmed Requiem.

'So—let's get down to business. Is Brezhenko dead or alive, Walter?'

'Well, it's puzzling. We've had reports that he made an appearance at the Central Committee meeting on Wednesday;

but our agent, Birch—God, is that damn machine switched off?—tells us he's dead. And he's always been reliable.'

O'Reilly stared at the TV screen, which showed a tall, aged man standing at a podium. 'Isn't that Finn?'

'That's right,' murmured Shrub. 'Receiving the Peace Prize in Oslo, I guess.'

'So he could be dead or he could be alive,' growled O'Reilly, drumming blunt fingers on the desk. 'Turn the sound up, Shrub. Drown those fucking yellow-bellies.' He nodded towards the window, through which floated the never-ceasing shouts of demonstrators and the wail of sirens. Shrub turned up the sound, and they heard the cool yet impassioned tones of Stanislav Finn. Finn, as old as the century, carried an unparalleled moral authority. A one-man non-aligned country, he had worked tirelessly all his life to make the United Nations what it is. The award to him of the Nobel Peace Prize had received almost universal approbation; indeed, seemed too long delayed. Whatever he said, wherever he spoke, his words carried weight. The four men in the Oval Office, sipping scotch, watched and listened intently.

· 2 ·

I am signally conscious of the honour you are bestowing upon me, and of my unfitness for it. When I think that one of my predecessors is my old friend Menachem Begin, at whose side I stood as we watched the Hotel David burning in Jerusalem—then I squirm in my inadequacy! But thank you. Thank you.

Speaking of that liberation struggle in Palestine after the war takes my mind back, of course, to one of the most arduous, yet exciting and rewarding, periods of my life, when my Jewish friends were, so to speak, on the other side. I had the good fortune to be at such camps as Auschwitz, Sobibor, Dachau, Belsen, Birkenau, Maidenek, Treblinka. In my small way I was able to help ease the problems of overcrowding in those camps; yet it was never easy to make the selection. There are times, however, when all one's efforts seem worthwhile. I remember, as though it were today, a cold, clear, peaceful morning in Auschwitz, the ground covered in a layer of snow, the smoke from the chimneys scarcely hazing the mild blue sky—and an air of serene quietness. Such memories—forgive me—are more precious to me even than the award of medals and honours.

Your citation makes special mention of the late 1930s, my work with the SS and the NKVD; and those were indeed eventful and arduous years. Looking back, I'm not sure how I got through them—only, I suspect, because I was still relatively young and strong. All that constant rushing about between Berlin and Moscow and the Siberian wilderness . . . Not to mention trips to China and elsewhere—I can't imagine how I did it! I do know that, even though I have the constitution of an ox, I was often totally exhausted. There never seemed any respite. Earlier, there had been the pacification of the Russian *kulaks*, so immensely painful; and, still before that, the Russian revolution and civil war, the world war, the pacification of the Armenians in Turkey . . . Yet when you're in your teens and early twenties, anything seems possible.

After the fighting in Palestine, and the partition of India, I was tempted to put up my feet and call it a day. But one can't so easily, if one has any ideals, escape one's responsibilities. Africa called; Vietnam, Cambodia . . . And there is still no rest. Much remains to be done in the Middle East, in Northern Ireland . . . And there are countries as yet almost untouched, such as Canada, New Zealand, and your own Scandinavian lands. At times, as one looks around the world, one is inclined to despair. Yet I think one can look back on small successes. I think one can say there is no longer a serious Armenian problem in Turkey; no longer a Red Indian problem in America—but that, in no small measure, was due to my father; no longer a Jewish problem in Europe; no longer a Palestinian problem in Israel. Lebanon and Iran are rich in promise. So is South Africa. If I have served the cause of peace in these areas, I have not lived my life in vain.

I count myself lucky to have known some of the great men of our century; indeed, been close friends with several of them. Hitler, Beria, Stalin, Eichmann, Franco, Mengele, Pol Pot, Khomeini, Gadaffi—these are a few that come to mind.

But infinitely more valuable have been the friendships I've made with ordinary folk; the shared comradeship of a guerrilla dug-out—that kind of thing. These are friendships that never fade. One of the greatest joys of my declining years is to hear, out of the blue, from someone lost to sight for decades, yet never forgotten. A few months ago, for example, I happened to be giving a lecture in Brisbane. A few days later, a letter reached me at my hotel. I'd like to read it to you. It's just a simple straightforward letter, from a simple uneducated man; yet it really tells us everything about this struggle for peace in which all decent people are engaged . . .

'Forgive an old Boer, who settled here in Queensland in 1910, but hearing you speak the other night brought back happy memories. You were a familiar and welcome visitor in my early days, and I once enjoyed a conversation with you. You probably won't remember me. But I can still see you, very clearly, in that green tank, with a red cross painted on the front, and you standing very erect in it, your face stern and streaked with sweat (you must excuse my blunt language). The Abos from round Warata used to have a special language when talking to their mother-in-laws—I don't know if you were aware of that fact. It's of no particular moment, but I always thought it was funny. They're not very bright, and it must have been an awful waste of what little intelligence they have to learn two languages, one for their mother-in-laws and one for everyone else. Anyway, you mentioned in your talk the Warata massacre, and said you thought one coon had escaped from it. That's true. I know him. His name is Dick One-Eye, and he's still alive, living in an old coons' home on Palm Island. He lost an eye in the episode, before slipping into the bush. That's what he told me, but most of them are liars. It's just as likely he lost it in a quarrel with his wife or mother-in-law.

'Well, like I said, forgive an old Boer for rambling on. I've spent a lot of my life travelling the world. In fact, our paths met up again in Bolivia in about 1950. You did a lot of good work with the tribes of the Amazon jungle, which I've never seen mentioned very much. I'd like to back up what you said about the young people of today, it's all drugs and foul language. It wouldn't surprise me one bit if the end of the world was approaching, as we near the year 2000, not that I suppose I'll see it. I'm living alone here, since my dear wife passed on, with my mother-in-law and one python for company. She's a good few years younger than me, because my wife was a lot younger. I don't get in to Brisbane much, but when somebody told me you were speaking there, I just had to make the trip. It was the flying doctor, he was seeing me for my gout, which is very bad just now, so I hope you will understand if I don't make this too long, but I can picture so vividly that green tank with the red cross on it, and you standing up in it, tall and gaunt and stained with sweat, driving on through the jungle, the trees and canes crashing and a trail of flattened Abos, yes and I've seen a few of their women burn, though it's not to be recommended in the dry season because of the risk of bush fires. The Abos round here use the female case for anything which is on fire, according to Dick One-Eye, but like I said you can't believe a word he says.

Yours cordially,
'Jan Viljoen'

Well, as I warned you, it's a very simple but very honest letter, and it moved me greatly. Of course I remembered him! If my memory serves me correctly, he was with us on that day when we pacified Warata. I'd been speaking of it in my lecture. I'd referred to the coon who got away, but said we'd shot eleven of them, men and children; and then raped the women before pouring kerosene over them and setting light to them. Yet it's surprising how memory can play tricks; I was convinced we had raped all the women, but someone in the audience reminded me that a couple of the women were not raped in the accepted sense of the word. We had simply ejaculated into their mouths. And also, two or three of the women were raped anally as well as vaginally. No one else remembered one of the lads escaping into the bush, so it was fascinating to have it confirmed by Jan Viljoen, my old friend.

I suppose one can chalk up Australia too as a success. There is no aboriginal problem there now, to any degree. But there is still so much work to be done. There are thousands of people alive today who have never looked with terror down the barrel of a gun; women and young girls who have never been forced to open their legs at knifepoint —for whom a can of kerosene is merely a primitive form of fuel for cooking. I am old, and cannot do everything.

Having said all that, I am, I repeat, conscious of the worth of this honour bestowed on me today. I accept it on behalf of my fellow workers, past and present—the little people who have played their part in striving for peace—like Ken Viljoen. I thank you, my friends, from the bottom of my heart.

(Applause)

· 3 ·

'Do you *have* to show those, Hank?'

'I shouldn't worry. They've lost any shock value they may have had, Walter.'

Walter Mako stood with Hank Klondyke, America's most respected political interviewer, in the Oval Office. They were watching a monitor on which was appearing documentary footage of Nicaraguan and Salvadorean atrocities.

Mako was in a green tracksuit, having just come from a jog. Klondyke wore a jacket and tie. Around the two men surged, in apparent chaos, cameramen and assistants, setting up Klondyke's presidential interview.

'And we'll be showing these when I ask the President about the First Lady's modelling.'

A sequence of sepia-tinted stills appeared. In the first, a blonde wearing a tight-belted 40s-style skirt and sweater was coyly adjusting a garter strap; in the last, she was down to cami-knickers. Mako groaned. 'God, Hank! Give the old man a break!'

Klondyke shrugged. 'You're the one who asked us to spare

the guy's face. We have to show the viewers something.'

'Couldn't you,' said Mako, 'let the cameras kind of roam around the office? Demonstrate the historicity of the place, the weight of tradition?'

'We'll be doing that. But for Chrissake, you can't be showing an ornament while the President is explaining why his wife posed for cheesecake pictures forty years ago! Look, they've been in *Playboy* and every news broadcast in the country! Everybody's had their smirk and their coarse joke, Walter. They're starting to think now, She was a helluva goodlooking girl, and what was the harm? A hard-up kid in Hollywood who made a few bucks to send to her poor old momma! That's what they're starting to think! Just be thankful she didn't show her pussy!'

Both of them grinned; Mako, ruefully.

'But,' continued Klondyke, 'if you'd like us to focus more on the old man's face . . .'

'Hell, no. It's all shot up. He looks a wreck. I'll trust your judgement. Do your best for him.'

'You know I will,' said Klondyke smoothly. 'I love the guy. I don't want to see him impeached.'

'Thanks.' Mako slapped the veteran interviewer on the back. 'I'd say this is his last chance, Hank. Finn's attack at UNO last night was just about the final straw. So help him come across in his true colours—as a decent, sincere, clean-living and peace-loving guy; and if he's told a few white lies, it was only to try and save other people's necks.'

'Trust me.'

'Take it slowly. He doesn't respond as quickly as he used to do.'

Klondyke patted his shoulder. 'I know my job. Don't worry.'

The door opened and O'Reilly strode in. He seized Klondyke's hands and shook them warmly.

'How are you, Mr President?'

Klondyke led him to an armchair, sat him down; took the chair placed nearby.

'Good to see you, Hank!'

A fluttery girl assistant fumbled a mike on to O'Reilly's tie. Mako, leaning over the President, whispered: 'Mr President, your only hope is to be completely frank and open.'

'I specially asked for you, Hank.'

'I'm honoured, sir. Now, could you give us a level? Could you say something?'

Mako stepped back. O'Reilly's eyes—two slits of red withdrawn into puffy bags—followed him. 'I intend to be completely frank and open.'

'Thank you,' said Klondyke. 'That's fine.' His eyes followed the monitor, as it showed the lead-in to the interview. 'We're live as from—now . . .'

Mako slid his frame into the small control room, next door. He perched on a vacant chair and stared, in company with the production team, at the monitors.

An outside shot of the White House turned to a corner of the Oval Office, the two men sitting in relaxed and lonely companionship.

'That's beautiful!' murmured the producer. 'He looks very relaxed.' The camera focused on Klondyke, grey-haired, dignified, suave. Mako strained forward.

K: Mr President, for the first time since the Bolshevik revolution, Russia has a young leader, by all accounts an energetic leader. In the circumstances, wouldn't it have been wiser for you yourself to have attended Comrade Brezhenko's funeral, rather than Vice-President Shrub?

O: Sure! The only good Commie's a dead Commie!

K: Pardon me?

O: No, I don't think so, Hank.

K: I'm not sure I follow you.

O: You want me to speak louder? I have a cold. Maybe old Brezhenko's bug wanted to emigrate and got a lift with Shrub! Oh, we're on the air? Fine . . . Well, no; it would have been impolite not to have seen Prince Diana and Princess Charles off. I don't think a funeral's a good time to get acquainted with someone.

K: How do you see yourself handling Comrade Grobichov when you finally get to meet him?

O: What don't you follow?

K: I'm sorry; our lines seem to be crossed, Mr President. How would you deal with Grobichov?

O: Maybe I could teach him a thing or two!

K: He appears to have made an impression on the Vice-President . . .

O: He's just a greenhorn!

K: The Vice-President?

O: So he says. Well, time will tell.

K: I'm not sure we're speaking the same language . . . Never mind—I'd like to move on to this crisis in your Presidency which has become known, however much we might prefer a more dignified title, as Jerkoff. For the second time in a decade, an administration has been shaken to its roots by a scandal which seemed to begin with something of small moment. In your case, Mr President, an interview you gave to the Russian poet Surkov. The hostility you have aroused is broadly of two kinds. On the left, people are describing you as a warmonger. On the right— if you will forgive the pun—as a whoremonger. Your aggressive responses to questions about the superpower relations have gravely impaired the NATO alliance. Your prurient responses —as it appeared to many—to questions about your private life have shocked your natural constituency. On all sides there is resentment at what is seen as a cover-up, in the course of the various statements made by you and members of your White House team. I hope tonight, Mr President, we can get to the truth of the matter finally. I know you very much want to lay it on the line. So can we begin with the personal matters, some of which involve the First Lady too. I'll ask you bluntly—has the First Lady entertained a lover at Camp David?

O: Not the Vice-President.

K: I don't think anyone ever imagined—

O: Shrub's no greenhorn! Whenever he's had to stand in for me, he's always performed very capably.

K: You mean he *has* slept with the First Lady?

O: Hank, people imagine all sorts of things! The whole purpose of this interview tonight is to shed a little reality.

K: What you want to get across, surely, is that you and your wife have had a long and faithful marriage for almost forty years?

O: Hell, no!

K: Oh—I'm sorry. In that case you won't mind me asking, equally bluntly—did you commit adultery with Irma Fleming?

O: Yes. Absolutely. For forty years, Hank, and with luck there'll be another forty.

K: Well, no one can accuse you of not being frank with us tonight, sir. It may be almost unnecessary to bring this up, after what you've told us, but—yes, these notorious pin-up photos—you can see them on the monitor—originally published in a girlie magazine called *Upskirt* in, I think, 1940: I imagine the First Lady wouldn't deny that she's the model? Have you anything to say about them?

O: No. Absolutely not. I'm trying to be completely hank, Frank. I'm sorry, I mean frank, Frank. Hank. I'm afraid the lady has been telling a few fibs.

K: Okay, I guess that's enough about that. My own view, and that of a lot of Americans thank God, is that your morals and your wife's morals are your own affair. But when it comes to matters of war and peace, it's very much everyone's affair. During the crisis, the United States has become heavily involved in military action in Central America. Scenes like these take our minds back to the Vietnam war . . .

O: Yes, I see them. Well, they were tastefully shot. You must bear in mind they were very poor, Hank. You need a few bucks in your purse to be refined. Americans aren't prissy. Good God, we have full-frontal nudes on cable TV! It's 1982, Hank! I'd call them just harmless cheesecake. Even rather artistic. The guy who shot them knew his stuff.

K: I must confess—looking at those scenes—I find your answer somewhat blood-chilling. What do you say to those critics who've accused you of being sadistic? Obviously I'm thinking also of the letter a New York call girl claims you wrote to her when you were a senator. Did you do those things?

O: If something has to be done, I don't believe in pussy footing around.

K: Mr President—would you ever launch a first strike?

O: I'll be very frank with you, Hank. There are times when you have certain fantasies. Everybody has them—we don't need Freud to tell us that. But it doesn't mean you'd carry them out. I've had fantasies, because I'm only human, but I don't go around putting them into action, I assure you.

K: Mr President, don't you think the time may have come for you to resign?

O: No.

K: Are all your faculties intact?

O: No, Hank. I intend to go on fighting for peace and our great country.

K: Thank you.

O: I've never felt fitter. I want to assure the people of the United States—

K: We're off the air, sir.

O: Thank you.

K: Do you mind if I smoke?

O: Oh . . . Well, I guess that cleared the air, Hank. Thanks!

· 4 ·

'What's happened to our President,' suggested Dr Mordecai Greenbaum, addressing a group of trainee analysts in Brooklyn, 'is quite moving and profound. It's a breakthrough into his own reality. All his life he's lied, like all politicians; now he can't take it any more. He's cursed with the need to tell the truth at all times, even though he knows he's going to be hounded by the whole world as a result. Klondyke was completely thrown, because he's used to evasions and lies. Right away O'Reilly had to admit he'd have enjoyed the Brezhenko funeral because another Communist was dead. Well, we know this is true; we just don't expect our President to come out with it. Then, he's tired of covering up on his sex life. He's the first President who's told it like it is. He's been screwing Irma Fleming for forty years, and he's proud of it. He's no intention of stopping. The Great American Public is terribly shocked, even though two-thirds of them are screwing their neighbours' wives and husbands and intend to go on doing so. Or else they're on their fifth or sixth partner, having muttered a few phrases of legalistic jargon before a judge to give a gloss to their adulteries. Similarly with Wanda O'Reilly: he can't be bothered to pretend Shrub hasn't been screwing her. Maybe it's tough on Shrub, but it's happened, it's no big deal, O'Reilly says he gives her a good screw. We should be saying, That's fine, I'm glad they've had some good times together. Instead, Shrub gets it so hot he has to resign. It's crazy!

'The public are hypocrites. All the men have slept with whores, sometime in their life, and all the women have sold their bodies for gain, whether it's a nice dinner, or a mink, or marriage with a guy with a fat bank balance. All of us, like O'Reilly said, have had fantasies of tying a woman up and beating the shit out of her—or being abused in that way—even if we haven't, as he did, written a letter about it, saying what we'd like to do. I guess all of you have imagined what it would be like to be the President and have that awful power at your fingertips. You just have to press a button, as easy as fingering a girl's clit—and wham, the world's vanished! Except you, cosy in your bunker! Think what it's like to *be* the President. He's bound to fantasise that a thousand times a day. O'Reilly's had the courage to admit it, and so he's become the world's most hated guy, a prisoner in the White House!

'And those peasants shot up by our peace force in Nicaragua . . . When we first saw those pictures, which of us didn't experience a thrill of excitement? We couldn't bear to admit it, of course, even to ourselves, so we covered it over with compassion and outrage. But essentially we felt like O'Reilly. They were just poor peasants, thousands of miles away; really we couldn't give a shit about them. A few less mouths to feed. And the photographs were beautiful. He's right about that too; they're art; they've won prizes. But also he was dead right to use that term "cheesecake". At first they shocked us, but now when we see them we feel a gentler titillation, like seeing those pictures of Wanda.

'In your encounter groups, you'll be working to get your

clients to strip themselves as naked as O'Reilly's done. It isn't easy. It's kind of frightening when it happens to the President. Eliot said, "Humankind cannot stand very much reality"; and maybe we can't stand it at all in our President, maybe they're right to impeach him. I'd feel safer with Mako, who knows how to lie. But you can't help admiring O'Reilly; he's suddenly, from being a banal idiot, touched greatness . . .'

Mordecai Greenbaum glanced around his group challengingly. Their heads were bowed in attitudes of serious reflection. A middle-aged woman, squatting crosslegged in faded knee-length jeans, broke the silence:

'Yeah, I can see that's true. I have orgasmic dreams about pressing the button. But I don't agree with what you said at the end. Surely the world would be a lot safer place if all the world leaders were honest and open like O'Reilly. Why should we throw out an honest President?'

Others murmured assent. But a fat man in a tee-shirt marked O'REILLY WATCHED ME AND WANDA said, 'I can't go along with it. What sort of a guy says people were shot tastefully?'

'I thought he was kind of needling the viewers at that point,' responded the woman in knee-length jeans. 'Being ironic.'

'I agree with Linda,' said Dr Greenbaum; and the group of trainee analysts launched into a lively discussion.

· 5 ·

I have attained the highest power.
BORIS GODUNOV

'Wouldn't it be the most honourable course, Mr President?
Wouldn't it be better than being dragged to Capitol Hill, like
Cleopatra through the streets of Rome?'

Defence Secretary Requiem sat in the Oval Office, looking
down compassionately at O'Reilly. The President was on his
knees, weeping and shaking. He had finally cracked. Requiem,
a fervent Baptist, had prayed with him and for him.

'Be strong, Mr President. It will take courage, but I know
you can do it. Don't go down in history as the President they
impeached.'

O'Reilly responded with more desperate sobs.

'Do it, Tiger! You don't mind me calling you that? You *are*
a tiger . . . Preserve your honour, I beg you. Don't become a
cartoon figure of shame. What I'm suggesting is right, you
know it in your bones.'

The Tiger went on weeping, his great shoulders heaving.
Requiem rubbed a thumb behind his glasses and sighed. 'Don't
fight it, Mr President. It's God's will. Launch a first strike.'

O'Reilly's sobs were easing, he was crying himself out like

a tired unhappy child. Requiem changed his tone subtly, as a parent's tone changes when a child's fit of grief is ebbing.

'You know it's logical. Communism is the ideology of Satan. And Satan is winning. He owns almost all of Asia; he's going to get Central America, and South America is only a matter of time. Even the Catholic priests are fighting on his side down there. We shall become isolated. Godless Communism will besiege us, and we won't be able to hold out.

'You can save the world for God with one press of a button. Truman could have done it simply by threatening to use the Bomb, before the Soviets had it; but then, Truman was a secret Communist himself. Regrettably, it can only be done now by using the power. I don't like the idea of all the deaths and destruction; but the future will bless you for it, and the Lord will reward you for it. We have enough missiles to wipe out Russia and also the Chinese launch sites. There's a good chance Grobichov won't respond at all. Nobody's ever believed it would actually happen—not really. He's new, and he'll panic. He may think, We're doomed anyway, so what's the point in annihilating millions of Americans? What does Hamlet say? "Conscience doth make cowards of us all." I remember you telling me you weren't sure, if it came to it, you could press that button. But more likely he'll hope it's a terrible mistake, that their technology has screwed up; and he'll go on hoping that till it's too late to respond. I calculate a four-in-ten possibility Russia will be obliterated without firing a single missile back.

'If that happens, think what a triumph you'll have, Mr President!' Requiem laid an affectionate hand on O'Reilly's shoulder. 'But supposing they do launch a second strike. America will be in an awful mess, that's true. But the command structure will be intact. The blow won't be mortal; our infrastructure is stronger than theirs. Besides that, the southern hemisphere will be untouched; and that's firmly democratic.

Power will rest with us, together with Australia and New Zealand, South Africa, Argentina, and Brazil. Inside twenty years—which is a mere eye-blink in human history—the planet will be flourishing again, democracy will be everywhere triumphant. And we can outlaw nuclear weapons. We can destroy what will be left of ours, because we won't need them; there won't be a single tyrant on the earth. Peace will prevail.'

Requiem halted. O'Reilly kneeled in stillness, his head bowed. Sensing a turning-point, a moment of decision, the Defence Secretary pressed his hand firmly on the President's shoulder. 'Think it over, Tiger,' he said gently.

A phone rang. The red phone. Both men almost jumped out of their skins. O'Reilly crawled across the floor, pulled himself up, and lifted the phone.

'Yes, it's the President.' O'Reilly wiped his eyes with a sleeve. 'Yes. Yes, I agree.'

He replaced the receiver. He turned on Requiem a dazed and wondering look. 'It's a miracle, Henry!' he said huskily. 'Your prayers have been answered! We're saved. It was Grobichov. He wants a summit!'

'He'll be crucified, Henry. We've got to stop it.'

'But we've tried everything. He's determined to go. He and Wanda. There's no way they can get an Impeachment Bill on the statutes in time.'

'I know that.' Mako groaned. 'And he insists on having fifteen minutes alone with him! Just think what those fifteen minutes could do to the free world!'

'You don't have to tell me, Walter.'

'Henry, I'm having terrible thoughts. I've never favoured political assassination. Not even for Castro or Gadaffi. But I'm beginning to think there comes a time . . .'

Requiem's lenses flashed. 'Don't say another word, Walter. It would come out, eventually. It always does.'

'I know, I know. I'm sorry. We'll just have to go through with it. We'll cut the fifteen minutes down to five. He can really only say hello in that. And you and I will be at the table with him.'

'That's right. It'll be okay. We'll damp down expectations.'

'Well, there's a groundswell of feeling that he's foxed the Reds—scared them with a show of irrationality. *Time*, I hear, is coming out with the headline *Has Groucho outsmarted Karl?*'

'Jesus fucking Christ!' Mako groaned. 'I'm sorry, Henry.'

Requiem, blushing, smiled. 'I think Christ might forgive you at this moment in time.'

· 6 ·

Air Force One droned through the ether. The presidential party had dined well and everyone felt sleepy. From time to time Wanda O'Reilly pressed her wrinkled but still pretty face to the window, hoping to catch a glimpse of ice-blue Atlantic or French chateaux; but the white carpet of clouds persisted. Sipping a Bloody Mary, she felt relaxed for the first time in weeks. The Jerkoff scandal had been hell. Even after Grobichov's invitation had taken the pressure off slightly, she'd had to cope with Christmas arrangements and order designer clothes for the summit. No one had seen Grobichov's wife, but she was rumoured to be rather smart and attractive; and she was bound to be at least ten years younger than Wanda. In the wake of the dampening down of expectations for nuclear arms reduction, the press had speculated endlessly on who would win the fashion battle, she or Mrs Grobichov. Well, Wanda had chosen her outfits; she could do no more; it was in the lap of the gods.

So she could recline deeply, and chat to Tiger about family matters. O'Reilly made brief, grunted replies. Simultaneously he browsed through the latest *Readers' Digest*, and tried to take in what Mako, on his right, was saying. Mako was trying to coach him on the number and disposition of Soviet missiles. It was desperately late in the day to be doing so, on the eve of the Geneva summit; but O'Reilly had made himself incommunicado for the past two weeks, saying his family Christmas was sacred.

Mako's belated briefing was not going particularly well. The President had little idea of the number and disposition of American missiles, let alone Soviet ones. Yet, unlike a previous president, who had found it a problem to walk and chew gum at the same time, the Tiger gave no impression of being overstretched by the buzz of voices at each side.

Vaguely he heard Wanda speak about little Tim, their six-year-old grandson. She thought he'd enjoyed Christmas at their ranch. What had he been up to, she enquired, on the last evening, when he'd dragged his grandad off to the playroom?

Mako was wishing the Americans had something up their sleeve, to set against Grobichov's offer of a fifty per cent reduction in missiles. Some way of exerting pressure.

O'Reilly, his eyes scanning the *Is Your Slip Showing?* quips, murmured, 'Uhhuh, uhhuh,' to both parties. Then he laughed raucously. 'That's a good one! Read that!' He leaned leftwards, thrusting the magazine at his wife, stubbing a finger at the joke. She smiled and handed the magazine back. 'Oh, he was making up a computer game. He wanted me to see it. It was way above my head.' He veered to the upright, went on browsing.

'That's amazing!' Wanda exclaimed. 'A computer game, at his age! What's he calling it, what's it about?'

'If we could exploit our technological advantages . . .' reflected Mako. 'Any ideas, Mr President?'

'Shoot-Out. Anti-matter rays in space, which knock out nuclear missiles as soon as they're launched.'

'Gracious!' said Wanda. 'And could it work?'

Mako frowned. 'It sounds pretty science fictional. It hardly sounds like a practical proposition.'

O'Reilly inclined his head; his reading glasses slid down a centimetre. 'Reuben's tested it on the big MIT computer. He says it's absolutely viable.'

Mako: 'Your son-in-law? Well, I'll be damned!'

Wanda made a proud, crooning noise. 'What a kid! Of course he takes after his father in that way.' Reuben Klein was America's leading physicist, a Nobel Prizewinner. 'It just bothers me a little he shuts himself away so much. He ought to have a brother or sister. But they don't want any more kids.'

O'Reilly hooted; his head shot back. 'Boy, that's a good one!' Drawing out a silver fountain pen, he drew an asterisk. He'd try it on Grobichov, see whether the guy had a sense of humour.

'Katie's changing her method of birth control,' Wanda continued. 'She thinks she's been on the pill long enough, and I guess she's right. They considered a vasectomy, but Reuben won't have it. She thinks he's being very selfish.'

Mako came out of deep reflection to say, 'Grobichov would hit the roof, you know that! So would a lot of our bleeding hearts. They'd say it was too dangerous.'

'Selfish?'

'Well, and selfish, yes. A defensive system they didn't share. Of course we could say we intend to share it with them, when it's ready. At a price . . .'

'Uh-huh. Well, you know he *is* pretty selfish, Tiger. Anyway, she's going to get herself fitted with an IUD . . .'

O'Reilly chuckled; penned another star.

'I'm not so sure I like that name Shoot-Out,' crooned Mako. 'It sounds too aggressive, don't you think? We need something less flamboyant.'

'IUD?'

'Intra-uterine device,' Wanda explained. 'It's fitted in the womb.'

'IUD?' Mako's brows knitted. 'Oh, I get it! Independent Unilateral Defence?'

O'Reilly gave a brief nod of understanding. 'It sounds painful.'

Mako nodded, chuckling drily. 'But a wonderful name, sir! Perfect! It's a kind of contraceptive, after all! IUD . . . Great!'

Though hard of hearing, Wanda caught the echo of her own speech. She pulled herself forward, glancing across at the Secretary of State. 'IUD?' she asked.

Mako leaned forward, turning towards her. 'Yes—did you get all that? Isn't it a great idea, and a great title? Independent Unilateral Defence!'

Wanda, blushing faintly, smiled. 'That's a good one!' She nudged her preoccupied husband. 'You should use that on Grobichov, darling!'

'Oh, we are,' said Mako. 'Or rather we're going to offer him a share.'

She frowned. 'A share?'

Mako nodded, then excused himself, saying he wanted to talk about it to the other guys before he got carried away by the idea. He slid out of his seat.

'Walter wants us to share the IUD with the Russians,' O'Reilly explained. 'Show them we won't be selfish with our technology.'

Her frown cleared. 'Oh, I get it! Well, that's a great idea. In fact now you mention it, I've read about their primitive birth control. Most women just have to have abortions. It would be a very humanitarian gesture, Tiger.'

Reading, he shook his head in amused disbelief. 'There's a guy in a New York asylum who thinks his wife's head is a hat! Jesus!'

'Yes, I read that article,' Wanda said. 'When their nerve cells go, or something. Awful!'

'I didn't know that. Well, we must help them.'

As an obsequious waiter started clearing away glasses for the descent, Mako slid back in his seat. He looked flushed, triumphant. 'Requiem and Bloomfield are very excited about this, Mr President!' Wanda O'Reilly craned forward to listen. 'Bloomfield was dubious, until I told him your son-in-law had tested it and it could work. Like Bloomfield said, if Klein thinks it'll work, it'll work.'

'Oh, you were discussing—'

Mako nodded. 'Yes. Isn't it fantastic, Wanda! Anti-matter rays that can knock out nuclear missiles from space!' He smiled at O'Reilly whose lips were moving silently as he read. 'What a brain he's got!'

'He takes after his father,' Wanda said.

'Oh, really?' Mako's mind flashed to O'Reilly's father, a toothless incontinent ex-bricklayer in a Washington rest home.

'Well, and his grandad too.' Smiling, she pecked a kiss on her husband's rough cheek. 'You can't imagine how inadequate I feel when he's around, Walter.'

'No, no,' said Mako gallantly. 'You have the beauty.'

Her wrinkled, rouged cheeks reddened further. 'You're too kind!'

O'Reilly cracked an exclamation. 'Jesus! And there's a guy whose brain sees things after his eyes have moved on! He'll enter a bedroom, reach the bed, then try to open the door!'

Mako leaned aside to glance at the *Digest*. Wanda, gazing out, gave a shrill cry: 'Look, Tiger! the Alps!'

Also approaching the Alps, from a north-easterly direction, was the Aeroflot which carried the General Secretary of the Communist Party of the USSR. Comrade Grobichov made no pretence of sharing his favours equally between the two ladies who flanked him. Throughout the journey he had virtually ignored the homely, Mongolian-featured, deeply wrinkled woman on his left, who gazed out of the window; his whole attention was directed at the beautiful, willowy blonde on his right. The young woman balanced a mass of documents in the lap of her slim black skirt, and from time to time she made a note with a Parker pen. Her shoulder nudged Grobichov's as they conversed. His eyes, fixed upon her, had a bulging, glistening, vulpine look.

She glanced down at a document, then raised her clear blue eyes to his again. She spoke rapidly; waited for him to collect his thoughts.

'If you are willing to pull away your Cruise and Pershing missiles from Europe,' Grobichov said in English, 'we will pull away from Europe our SS-20s.'

'*Khoroshó*,' the young woman said. 'But it's "pull out" not "pull away".'

Grobichov nodded and repeated, 'Pull out. Pull out your Cruise and Pershing missiles . . .'

'*Da*.'

'That's enough,' he said in Russian. 'Thank you, Larissa.'

Relaxing, straightening in her seat, she lifted the pile of documents in order to cross her legs, with a swish of black silken hose. She leaned her head back, closed her eyes.

Grobichov swayed, smiling, towards the contrasting figure on his left. His plump white hand touched her knee, which was covered by the cloth of heavy brown trousers. She turned from the window and exposed blackened teeth in a smile.

'How are you, you old cow?' he asked in English.

'*Shto eto szachit*, Alexei?'

'It means, Have you got over your travel sickness?'

'*Da, da*.'

'Good. Do you know, you have a face like a battleship?'

Still wearing her affectionate smile, she shook her head in a gesture of incomprehension.

Grobichov explained, 'You're going to stun the Americans.'

She exposed more black teeth, and her slit eyes widened in pleasure. 'Thank you. That's nice. I just hope I don't let you down, my dear.'

'You won't do that,' he said in Russian; adding in English: 'When God made you, Olga, he must have been pissed.'

The young blonde woman, opening her eyes, glancing with a barely disguised grin at Grobichov, said in English, 'Pissed is a vulgarism, I told you. Drunk would be better. You're cruel to her, Alexei!'

He chuckled. Addressing the frumpish woman again, he said, 'Larissa thinks my English is very good now, my dear.'

The woman, nodding and smiling, leaned foward to cast a friendly glance at the young *krasavitsa*, who said, 'Yes, he's a good student.'

The Mongolian-faced woman leaned back again, but jerked forward immediately, pressing her button-like red nose to the glass and digging her fingers into Grobichov's thigh. 'Look, my dear! The Alps! Oh, *chudno*!'

· 7 ·

Let me have your hand:
I did not think, sir, to have met you here.
ANTONY AND CLEOPATRA

In a room of the Chateau Belle de Nuit, the American head-quarters for the summit, O'Reilly and his chief aides had gathered for a final briefing before the arrival of the Soviet delegation. Mako stood by the window, staring at the sparkling lake fringed by birches. Beyond and above the lake and the birches, the shadows and light of a mountain revealed and concealed themselves as the cloudy sky permitted. Mako sipped coffee, as did Requiem and Bloomfield, both thin and spectacled, who perched on a sofa. The Tiger, holding a scotch on the rocks, drowsed in an armchair. Jetlagged, his puffy eyes were all but sealed over.

Requiem, eager and alert, said, 'IUD is the joker in the pack. It's going to sock them on the chin. It's a stroke of genius, Mr President. We should have known you'd have something up your sleeve! Of course they can never agree to accept it, so the result will be stalemate. We'll go ahead with it, keeping the offer open. That should disarm our domestic critics and our NATO partners. And when we've got IUD, the Reds will be helpless. That is, if you're correct in saying these weapons can knock out their missiles infallibly . . . You're sure about that?'

He stared at the President queryingly. O'Reilly, startled awake, said, 'Pardon me?'

'It's foolproof? These anti-nuclear rays?'

'They knocked them out on the MIT computer all right. According to my son-in-law.'

'That's great!' Requiem pressed his tiny hands together. 'What those boys can do!'

'It's foolproof,' O'Reilly confirmed.

'Then we'll have them over a barrel.'

O'Reilly gave a proud chuckle. 'You're right, Henry! It beats me how they do it. Mind you, these days they're given computers before they learn how to read. It helps, I guess.'

Requiem nodded. He glanced at his neighbour, Bloomfield, the nuclear arms expert. 'What do you say, Jake?

Bloomfield, stretching to put down his coffee cup, frowned. 'It sounds great in theory. Almost too good to be true. I'd be happier, though, if we knew a little more about it. I'd like to have talked to Klein personally.'

'Would it help to talk to him now, if we could reach him?' asked Requiem.

'That's no problem,' said O'Reilly. 'We could call him. What time is it?' He pushed back a stiff white shirt-cuff to glance at his watch. 'Two-fifteen. He'll still be at lunch in the faculty club at MIT.'

'No, it's morning there,' Bloomfield pointed out. 'I think Klein lectures early on Thursday mornings. But we might reach him before he goes in. I'll try his office.'

Bloomfield picked up a phone and dialled a dozen digits rapidly. 'Hi!' he purred. 'This is Bloomfield. We're in Geneva. Could you ring Dr Klein's number? Thanks.'

He waited. He held the phone towards O'Reilly. 'It might be better if you spoke to him first, Mr President.'

O'Reilly stretched forward to take the offered receiver. He listened. After a few moments he spoke in a hearty, over-friendly voice—the kind of voice one uses to a son-in-law: 'Is that you, Reuben? How are things? How are Katie and Tim? Look, speaking of that, I have Jake Bloomfield with me; he's curious about Shoot-Out, finds it hard to believe it'll work. Could you speak to him?' O'Reilly gave the phone back to Bloomfield.

Bloomfield, after saying 'Hi!' heard his Nobel Prizewinning colleague say, somewhat impatiently and sharply, 'Hi, Jake. Yes, it's perfectly practicable in theory; I've no reason to think it won't work, with a lot of time and a few bucks. Why do you want to know?'

'I can't talk about that right now, Reuben. I just wanted to hear it from your own lips. If you're sure it can work—that's good enough for me. You've sure been keeping it close to your chest! There'll be another Nobel in this.'

Klein's hollow, distant voice could be heard chuckling. 'Well, I like to keep them in the family. Though I think you may be exaggerating slightly! Have you met Grobichov yet?'

'No, he's due to arrive in about ten minutes.'

'Well,' said Klein, 'I have to teach some humble students. Good to talk to you, Jake.'

'See you soon.'

Bloomfield, putting down the phone, whistled through his teeth. 'Wow! He says it can definitely be done. What a break-through! The guy's a genius!'

Mako walked from the window to put down his empty coffee cup. His athletic frame straightened; he touched his chin with prayerful or thoughtful fingers. 'The problem now,' he murmured, 'is how to deal with this thing. We have no details about it, nothing specific. We should hold off on it till near the end. Spring it on them in the last session tomorrow.'

'You're right, Walter,' said Requiem. 'In any case, we don't want the summit to collapse as soon as it's started.'

'Spring what on them, exactly?' asked O'Reilly, gulping a final cube of bourbon-flavoured ice.

'The IUD,' said Mako patiently.

'This afternoon we'll concentrate on Soviet escalation, Afghanistan, and human rights. That should keep them busy.'

'Businesslike discussions!' Mako grinned, checking the time. 'The President should get out there ready.'

'You really think we should offer them the IUD?' O'Reilly said.

'Definitely. But only towards the end. Leave it to us. They'll probably stage a walk-out; then we'll announce the IUD plan, very generally, at a press conference, and say the Soviets have refused to accept our offer of collaboration.'

'An offer unequalled in history,' confirmed Requiem.

The President looked puzzled. 'You're quite sure they'll turn it down? I don't see why. We're only trying to help them control their population.'

He lifted a heavy eyebrow. His three aides laughed. Mako slapped the President on the back. He steered him towards the door. As they entered a large hall, security men gathered round them, O'Reilly's interpreter glided up, closely followed by the First Lady. She was in a green fur-trimmed coat and black suede boots. 'You look wonderful!' Mako complimented her warmly.

'Thank you!'

The President was being helped into his overcoat. Mako said, 'Mr President, could you bear to greet the Grobichovs without your coat?'

O'Reilly carried on sliding his arms in, but stopped when Mako repeated his request. 'Why, Walter?' he asked. 'It's ten below, out there.'

'I know. But it'll only be for a few minutes, sir. There are a million photographers out there, and pressmen, waiting to see how young and fit Grobichov looks compared with you. This summit is all about style. Whatever Grobichov's wife is like, Wanda can more than hold her own, I'm sure of that. He'll be wearing an overcoat; and if you show your toughness by waiting for him in your suit, you'll steal a march on him. You can be sure *they'll* have some tricks up their sleeve.'

As the President stood frozen, half-in and half-out of his overcoat, Wanda protested: 'You should have let us know before. He'd have worn thermals. He'll catch his death.'

'Okay,' grunted O'Reilly, slipping his arms out, straightening his jacket sleeves. He took Wanda's arm. The party moved towards the door.

· 8 ·

Crushed by and lost among a seething mob of news-hungry men, a deaf-mute female reporter for the London *Guardian* saw through a periscope O'Reilly's lips frame the words 'Fucking hell!' as he was staggered by the force of a frigid wind. His wife clutched on to him. His teeth clenched tight; he grinned and waved at the distant clapping crowd. The deaf-mute noted mentally his exclamation as the opening words of the summit; it became a scoop for the *Guardian* next morning, and one of the main talking points for newspapers and television studios throughout the free world. The news clampdown was total; reporters had to feed the multitude with less than the five loaves and fishes.

The deaf-mute also noted and reported that Wanda O'Reilly looked a great deal smarter than when she had walked, dowdy, from the plane. A thousand cameras flashed. Moments later, precisely at 2.30, a motorcade glided towards the chateau and came to a halt. Soviet security men swarmed from the limousines like ants from a crack. All eyes were on the third car, a gleaming black Zil, armour-plated, which had been brought in from Moscow. The multitude saw the great man step out: short, plump, rather stiff in movement, burdened by a heavy black overcoat and a black fur hat. Even from far away, the pressmen saw his teeth flash and his prominent eyes glisten pleasantly, as he stood waiting for his wife to step out. This was the big moment: was the mysterious Mrs Grobichov as attractive as rumour had it? Out of the limousine struggled a dumpy, wrinkle-faced woman wearing a shabby, shapeless grey coat, heavy-knit stockings and flat shoes. If she was younger than the President's lady, she disguised it well. The deaf-mute London reporter saw, if she did not hear, the gasps of surprise and derision expelled with the frozen breaths of her fellow journalists. Grobichov took his wife's arm, and walked with a defiantly lifted head towards the chateau steps. O'Reilly and his wife descended to meet them, smiling a welcome.

The President, lowering his gaze to the moon-like glistening-eyed face, thrust out his hand. Grobichov shook it: with reserve at first, then vigorously.

'Dobree deen!' said O'Reilly.

Grobichov glanced enquiringly at his interpreter. The man, bending close, said, '*Dobry dyen.*'

'Ah, *vy govoritye po-russki!*' Grobichov smiled up at the President.

'Good to meet you, Comrade Grobichov!'

O'Reilly's interpreter leaned towards him and murmured: 'Ah, you speak Russian.'

Grobichov gabbled in Russian, his smiling eyes never leaving O'Reilly's as their hands went on pumping. O'Reilly's interpreter leaned and murmured, 'You have an advantage over me.'

'I learned a few words, that's all,' O'Reilly explained. The Russian interpreter gabbled in Grobichov's ear. The Russian nodded and smiled, smiled and nodded. Their hands parted. 'Let me introduce you to Olga Ivanovna,' said the American interpreter, after another Grobichovian gabble. He was leading forward the dumpy woman, holding her by the elbow. She gabbled. 'Hello, Mr President,' said the American interpreter. O'Reilly shook her hand warmly. 'Good to meet you!' The Russian interpreter spoke in her ear, and she bared her blackened teeth.

Grobichov spoke again, and O'Reilly's interpreter said to him, 'My poor wife has a cold.'

'Let me introduce you to Wanda Wilburovna!' chuckled O'Reilly, turning and bringing his wife gently forward. As Wanda's gloved hand softly greeted Mrs Grobichov's woollen mitten, the Soviet interpreter, with a puzzled air, said, '*Pozvol'tye predstavit' vam Wandu Ueelburovnu.*' Grobichov shook his head in bewilderment as he grasped Wanda's hand. 'Her father's name is Wilbur,' O'Reilly explained with a smile. 'Just a joke.'

'*Shutka,*' explained the interpreter. Grobichov grunted, raised an eyebrow, looked sour; then, gabbling a sentence, spared the President's wife a wintry smile. O'Reilly's interpreter bent to her ear. 'It's colder than in Moscow—I'm glad to see that you're dressed more sensibly than your husband.'

O'Reilly turned to face the porchway, raising his arm shoulder high to guide his guests inside. 'It's getting a little chilly,' he said. 'Let's go in.'

'We'll have some tea and get acquainted,' said Wanda, taking Mrs Grobichov's arm. When her words were translated the Russian *babushka* muttered, '*Da, da! Spasibo!*'

The great doors shut behind them. 'We'll go in here,' said Wanda, indicating an open door. A waitress could be seen setting down a silver tray bearing a silver teapot, cups and saucers and a plate of American cookies. Seizing a passing aide's arm, Wanda hissed at him, 'Get the photographers in. And tell our people to make sure they get her to smile.' She rolled her eyes and the aide grinned. He too had seen and been gladdened by Mrs Grobichov's blackened teeth.

Meanwhile O'Reilly was following in Grobichov's wake as they were ushered towards an intimate salon for their brief head-to-head. Mako shouldered his way to O'Reilly's side. 'Remember, just five minutes,' he whispered.

'The guy has no sense of humour, Walter.'

Wanda had removed her coat, sat down, and placed her hand gracefully on the teapot-handle. Mrs Grobichov, declining to take off her shabby greatcoat, sat at the extreme edge of the *chaise-longue* they were sharing. Wanda, her smile brittle and poised, gestured to her to move closer. She did so. The crowded cameras flashed. Wanda poured the tea, and added slices of lemon.

'I don't blame you for keeping your coat on,' Wanda said loudly, and reporters' pencils scratched. 'It's colder in Geneva than in Washington.'

Two female interpreters had slid on to the *chaise-longue* beside the first ladies. The Russian repeated Wanda's words. The American passed on Mrs Grobichov's response: 'Yes, I'll take it off in a moment when I feel warmer.'

Wanda nodded, pretended to sip the tea. She hated tea. Her guest, raising her porcelain cup, gulped noisily. Her nose, too, gave a bark. Black hairs protruded from her nostrils.

'Where did you meet your husband?' Wanda asked, after a brittle pause.

'In Sverdlovsk . . . and you?'

'In Los Angeles.'

They nodded. Were silent. Mrs Grobichov crossed her legs at the ankles. Her shoes were lace-ups. Wanda stroked the soft suede of her left boot.

'My husband is a very nice man,' said Mrs Grobichov with a sigh. 'Already I am missing him.'

Wanda couldn't resist a smile. 'Well, he's not far away!' she remarked.

'It seems far.' The tired, yellowish eyes of the pleasingly

unattractive guest darted, frightened, around the high-vaulted room.

An aide caught Wanda's eye. She extended her hand. 'You're being taken back to rest now. I'm going to take a rest too. I'll see you again tonight—you're having dinner with us.'

'*Da. Spasibo.*'

'Wanda made these.'

'They are nice.'

The two men sat in adjoining armchairs, nibbling cookies.

'Is your wife a good cook, Mr Grobichov?'

'She is, but she has little time to do it. She's a Professor of Marxist-Leninist Psychology at Moscow University.'

'Uh-huh.'

'My wife is very clever and also very attractive; you will like her.'

O'Reilly's interpreter appeared to choke on a crumb as he translated 'very attractive', though he wasn't eating a cookie. He struggled to quell a grin.

'She must have a very high-powered mind. My son-in-law is a Physics professor.'

'Yes, I know that. Well, we must really work for peace in this short time, Mr President!'

'I'm sure I will.'

'You can be sure *I* will.'

Mako, stepping from the shadows, terminated the chat. The leaders leaned towards each other, their hands locked together. They smiled like pleasantly surprised, computer-dated lovers.

Ten minutes later, in the conference room, their relatives were finding all the hitches while the candidates for betrothal faced one another in sombre silence. Mako, Requiem and Bloomfield made unacceptable demands regarding the SS-20s, and wouldn't give an inch over Cruise and Pershing. Kirillov, Kropotkin and Bogdanovich made unacceptable demands regarding Cruise and Pershing, while not moving a centimetre over the SS-20s. The atmosphere became much more acrimonious when Mako shifted the discussion to human rights. Grobichov, talking too quickly for the translation to keep up, took control of his side. His fist hammered the table.

O'Reilly intervened only once—but with telling effect. 'Was it necessary,' he asked, 'to shoot Salkov-Shadrin, even if you suspected—quite wrongly—he was spying for us?' The heads of all four Soviets jerked back, their mouths fell open. It was several moments before Grobichov could stutter, 'He was not shot. Saltikov-Shchedrin was an embezzler, and deserved to be executed, but as a matter of fact he committed suicide before we could arrest him.'

Recovering, Grobichov was soon hammering the table once more, demanding to know when American blacks were going to get civil rights and when all Americans were going to be given a guaranteed job and proper health care.

He raged on. When at last he fell silent, no one spoke. Gloom descended on the conference room, matching the faded light through the windows and the keening wind off Lake Geneva.

His voice lower by an octave, Grobichov said, 'We have no point of contact. This is a waste of time.' He began gathering up his papers. Requiem and Bogdanovich did likewise.

'Comrade Grobichov,' said O'Reilly, 'I don't think we'll get much further like this. But why don't you and I take a little walk? Try to get to know each other better?'

The faces of O'Reilly's aides registered panic. 'Mr President—' Mako began to protest; but Grobichov interrupted, saying, 'Some fresh air might do us good. Yes, let's go.'

· 9 ·

They donned overcoats and mufflers, and set off to face the blast. A few lights twinkled from dusky lakeside villages; the shrouding sky showed a wash of pink in the west. Security guards flitted silently, invisibly, from tree to tree, following the two leaders as they trudged down a path. Grobichov almost slipped; O'Reilly clutched his arm. Their interpreters, just behind, had to check in order not to bump into them.

'*Spasibo.*'

'Thank you,' shouted the American interpreter into the wind. 'It should be a nice day tomorrow.'

The Russian shouted— '*Zavtra budyet khoroshaya pogoda.*'

'*Da.*'

They arrived at a small house on the verge of the lake. 'Shall we go in?' O'Reilly suggested. He threw open a door and ushered Grobichov in ahead of him. One of their shadows closed the door. They found themselves in a cosy, wood-beamed room; a fire roared in the hearth.

'Ah! someone's lit a fire!' exclaimed the President.

Wanda, O'Reilly knew, had checked out the lakeside house that morning and ordered the fire to be lit.

'*Eto priatno.*'

'This is nice.'

They doffed their coats and settled into rather uncomfortable armchairs.

And they talked. Haltingly and not without misunderstandings, but they talked. About their love for their own countries, their respect for the other's country. Grobichov, smoking a black Sobranie cigarette, even smiled at one of the President's jokes, when it had been explained to him. This relaxed the big red-headed American; Grobichov, for his part, felt himself warming a little to the affable personality of the man whose erratic, aggressive speeches had alarmed him and persuaded him that a meeting was advisable.

After some ten minutes of friendly though meaningless talk, the Russian leader pulled a notebook and pen from his breast pocket and adopted a brisker tone. Maybe they should forget the intractable problems for a while, he proposed, and talk instead about trade.

His beady eyes looked at the President quizzically. The American waited, his expression giving nothing away.

'It would help if you took a lot more of our exports, Mr President. Perhaps a twenty-five per cent increase.'

'I don't see why not. That's a good idea.'

Grobichov was startled. His voice purred: 'Well—excellent! We'll let our trade people deal with it, then?'

'I'm not so sure about that.'

Grobichov shrugged. 'Well, we can discuss it later. As long as you're agreed in principle.'

'Yes. We would like to help you with our technology. In particular, we'd like to sell you some IUDs.' Grobichov's interpreter looked puzzled. 'It's a contraceptive used by women,' O'Reilly explained. 'A plastic or metal loop fitted

into the womb. Katie, my daughter, is, having one fitted.
Wanda explained it to me last night. It's a pretty effective
contraceptive.'

After the Russian had listened to the lengthy translation, he
shrugged again. 'How many would you want to sell us?'

'In principle, yes. I've not much head for figures.'

Hesitating, struggling to comprehend, Grobichov's interpreter omitted the first sentence.

'Just a general idea, Mr President.'

'Who knows—twenty, thirty, million?'

Grobichov's eyes narrowed. His thoughts raced. He saw
a way of eliminating the problem of the rapidly increasing
non-Russian population. 'Well, it's possible,' he conceded. 'I've
nothing against it in principle. Of course, there's much more
important technology we're interested in. But enough for now.
You know, Mr President, I've been thinking—' He leaned
forward, touched O'Reilly on the knee—'This talk by the fire
has been very useful. Together, man to man, we can get on,
you and I. We need to protect each other against our officials.
Peace is too important to be left to that wrangling mob, yours
and mine.'

He broke off for the translation, his eyes keenly observing
O'Reilly. He pressed on at once, without waiting for a reply:
'I have a suggestion. Why don't we cancel tomorrow's round
table session, and you and I just meet here for an hour? We'll
get more done.'

'Why, that's great! It's settled! Let's shake on it!'

The Tiger thrust out his horny hand, and the Russian pumped
it exuberantly, exclaiming: 'It shall be the fireside summit!'

'I like it! I'll tell Mako and his cronies to get lost!'

'And I'll do the same with my team! Just you and I!'

'The fireside summit!' O'Reilly chuckled.

'*Da.*'

Beaming, still pumping the American hand, Grobichov

stood up. 'Now I must go back to the city and see how my wife is. I hope her cold won't stop her from coming tonight.'

'That will be great!'

'We look forward to it,' translated the Russian shadow.

'Good.'

'Yes, I'm sorry she has a cold,' said O'Reilly, as Grobichov helped him on with his overcoat. 'Tell her to wrap up warm.'

'I will.'

The wind, still colder with darkness, hit them again. The stars shone brilliantly. They walked arm in arm up the path, placing their steps with care.

'The weather has cleared,' said Grobichov. 'And our weather has cleared too, a little.'

O'Reilly's interpreter, his breath rasping, hurled the translation over his master's shoulder. Security men floated from tree to tree. When the small party reached the chateau, more flashbulbs exploded. Mako and Requiem hovered, with ill-concealed anxiety. Grobichov shook Mako's hand warmly, and checked that the photographers would be present again when he and his wife arrived at the O'Reilly residence for dinner. Sure, said Mako—just try to keep those guys away!

'*Khorosho*, Mr Mako. It's important the two couples are shown relaxing together, in friendship.'

'I couldn't agree more, Mr Grobichov.'

The leaders pumped hands again for the cameras, then O'Reilly and Mako waved the Soviet party off from the porch. The motorcade departed.

Once back in the building, Mako and Requiem grabbed their President. 'What happened?' they hissed.

'He's not such a bad guy.'

'What did you discuss?'

'Oh, we chatted for a while, about this and that. I kind of agreed we'd take more Soviet exports. And he agreed in principle to the IUD arrangement.'

'He *what*?' Mako stammered. Requiem's pale face grew whiter.

'He seemed pretty keen on it.'

'Did you explain what it was about, sir?' stuttered Mako.

'He knows what it means?' asked Requiem, his eyes bulging fish-like behind his glasses.

'Of course I explained. Now we must get back to our place. Are the limos ready?'

Amazement turning to incredulous joy, Mako and Requiem pummelled O'Reilly's shoulders. 'Well, I don't know how you worked it, Mr President! But it's wonderful news!'

'Boy oh boy!'

'Now let's drop it, you guys. I'm tired. I want a nap in my room before dinner.'

'You've earned it, Tiger!'

He was asleep, in a limo's soft upholstery, almost before the motorcade glided off.

· 10 ·

The Soviet motorcade, meanwhile, glided through the city outskirts, on a route closed to traffic. The Swiss, intent on buying or selling, paid little attention to the travelling circus. The Soviet leader sat in silence with his burly aide Bogdanovich, moustached, soldierly. At their side a security man cradled a sub-machinegun.

'Stop!' Grobichov barked: and the limousines and outriders, as if directed by a single will, slowed, moved in towards the kerb of a busy street, and halted. Grobichov pointed to a flower shop, and asked Bogdanovich if he would be so kind as to slip out and buy two dozen yellow roses. Bogdanovich complied, hurrying across the broad pavement towards the flower shop, followed by a discreet plainclothesman. The man with the sub-machinegun tensed forward, his finger crooked round the trigger.

Bogdanovich returned, clutching with embarrassment a huge bouquet of yellow roses. He climbed in, and the motorcade moved off. '*Spasibo*,' said Grobichov.

'*Nichevo*. For your wife?'

'*Da.*'

They rode in silence again for a time; then Bogdanovich, with a glance at the preoccupied security man, said quietly: 'Beautiful blossoms for a beautiful wife . . .'

'Thank you.'

Encouraged by his leader's friendly tone, the greying politician went on: 'You have staggered us all, by producing such a beauty! We'd heard she was attractive, but never dreamed she would be so lovely . . . We are all envious, Alexei!'

'Really? What's your wife like, Anatoli?'

By way of reply Bogdanovich shrugged his broad shoulders and pushed out his lower lip. 'But there is a very nice girl in Yalta . . .'

Grobichov grinned. 'I see! Naughty man! Naughty man! Well, I have no time for playing around, Anatoli. I stick to the mild domestic pleasures.'

'And with such a wife, I don't blame you. When did you meet her?'

'A long time ago,' said Grobichov, in a tone which discouraged his subordinate from asking any more personal questions.

'These are for you, my dear.'

Larissa glanced up from the bed, startled by his silent coming. She saw the brilliant bouquet. 'Ah, you're back,' she murmured. 'They're beautiful! Thank you.'

'I chose them to match your hair.'

Her hair, the colour of sunflowers, glowed against her pale complexion and the whiteness of her silk dressing gown. Yet it was questionable whether the gold of hair and roses outmatched the startling intensity of Larissa's blue eyes. Those eyes closed as her lips received his kiss. He straightened up, unbuttoning and taking off his overcoat.

'How have you been?' he asked.

'Bored.'

Freeing his plump neck from the tight collar and tie, he glanced at the book she had laid aside. 'Memories. Dreams. Reflections,' he murmured. 'What's that?'

'Oh, some Swiss psychologist. Jung. It's mystical rubbish. I was almost asleep.'

He perched on the bed, unlacing his shoes. 'Have you seen your mama?' he asked.

'Yes, she came in.'

'How did she find it?'

'I think she enjoyed it. How did it go?'

'Interestingly. He's friendlier than I expected.' He kicked off his shoes and stretched out beside her. She stroked his arm. 'Not aggressive. Maybe Kropotkin is right, and the whole Jerkoff affair was a big ploy to bring us to the conference table. He's clever. Yet also, at times, innocent, childish. I don't think his mind is in very good shape. You can see his eyes glazing over as he talks.'

'Could you understand him?'

'Yes, extremely well. He speaks slowly. At times I seemed to understand him better than my interpreter.'

'Good.'

He stretched towards his jacket, draped over a chair, and took a silver cigarette case and lighter from a pocket. After lighting a Sobranie, he leaned back against her stomach. Though she was naked under the silk gown, he didn't feel her muscles tense as he spoke of the contraceptives he'd agreed to buy. Her womb, as he ought to have known, was hungering to be with child; yet he went blundering on about how his aides suspected a trick. They thought the Americans might be planning to tamper with the metal or plastic uterine coils; introduce a poison, or—guessing the Russians would distribute them to their Moslem populations—a chemical for producing multiple births. The poison or chemical might be undetectable.

He said he was inclined to trust O'Reilly, at least on the contraceptives. They'd probably just manufactured too many.

'Maybe you could flirt with him a little tonight, darling,' he said, stroking her thigh absently. 'Test out his sincerity with your psychological acumen. And there's another thing—something very disturbing, shocking . . .' Grobichov pulled himself off the bed and took a few strides up and down: his face lowered and brooding, smoke curling from the black cigarette. 'Saltikov-Shchedrin may have been working for them.'

'Impossible.'

'O'Reilly let it slip, they thought we executed him for spying. Of course he denied in the same breath that he *was* a spy, but that was only to be expected. It really took the wind out of our sails.'

Larissa swung her legs off the bed and straightened up; she gazed into his eyes, shocked. Then her expression cleared. 'It can't be,' she murmured. 'He would hardly have risked exposure by embezzling state funds too.'

'Oh!' Grobichov chuckled grimly. 'He was no embezzler.'

'But he was charged with embezzlement, and shot himself to avoid scandal for his family. Surely?'

'Yes, he was *charged* with it.'

'You mean he was innocent?'

'As much as anyone in his position can be—yes.'

He sat down beside her, and stared at a blank wall. He recalled old Shchedrin's face as he, Grobichov, confronted him with the damning evidence; suggesting then a way out which would preserve his honour and a comfortable life for his wife and family. Grobichov felt Larissa sink back on to the bed beside him.

'But what a good thing he's dead!' he exclaimed. 'Just think —he could have been in power! And would have been if Brezhenko had had his way! A "Mole" for America, in the highest office!'

He stood up abruptly and resumed his pacing around. 'On

the other hand,' he murmured, 'it could be a clever ploy to upset us and have us turn the Kremlin inside out. It's the more likely, I guess. Let's hope that's the case. See what you can do with O'Reilly. You don't need to go to extremes; he'll be putty in your hands, my dear. An old man with an old wife and an old mistress . . . Who seems to have screwed around as much as Kennedy did . . . See what you can do . . .' He stubbed his cigarette butt. 'Wear your new dress and the corselette, Larissa. He likes bondage. When he puts his arm round you to take you in to dinner, he'll be a goner.'

While the Grobichovs were content to put up at, and with, the modest and undistinguished Soviet Mission, the O'Reillys and the top American aides enjoyed the luxury of staying at the mansion of a Jewish tycoon. The Weinstocks, friends of Henry Requiem, had generously moved out for the duration of the summit. Their marble mansion, the Maison Vichy, was situated a few miles westwards along the lake shore from the Chateau Belle de Nuit; as the American motorcade headed towards it, snaking around bends which threw up breathtaking images of snow-dappled vineyards and distant diaphanous mountains, the President slept as peacefully as a baby. Mako, Requiem and Bloomfield were also silent—not so much enjoying the scenery as meditating on the old man's amazing coup in getting the space defence initiative accepted.

Mako shook the sleeper awake as the motorcade drew into a pine-fringed drive. He nodded in drowsy agreement as the negotiators proposed that, after dining in their bedrooms, they meet up for coffee with the President and his guests. 'We'll gauge his attitude,' said Requiem; 'then plan our tactics for tomorrow's meeting.'

'That'll be fine.'

'Now have a good nap, Mr President,' Mako suggested as they climbed the marble steps to the entrance.

'That won't be necessary.'

They were greeted by agitated members of Weinstock's staff. The First Lady had been put to bed in a state of shock. And it was all because of O'Reilly's good nature.

Young Natan Weinstock's bedroom was being used by the President as his study. For the odd ten minutes, now and then, he would enter the cluttered room and sit down at the corner desk where the boy did his homework. And in return for young Natan's hospitality, the President had promised to provide his pet Mexican tarantula with fresh water. O'Reilly liked big spiders, and he had enjoyed letting the furry creature mountain-climb over his arm. Wanda, on the other hand, had a terror of spiders, and Tiger had thought it best not to inform her of the tarantula's presence.

On returning from the chateau, Wanda had gone on a tour of discovery. When, in the child's bedroom, she had seen the statuesque tarantula, amid plastic spacemen, she had assumed it was mercifully unreal. Then the obscene toy had moved, scurried across the carpet. Wanda's screams had brought security guards racing, guns at the ready; the spider, frozen again, had been clubbed to death.

The First Lady had been sedated; but she was still shuddering and crying when O'Reilly strode into their bedroom. He managed to soothe her eventually: but not until it was too late for him to have a proper nap. It was his fault that the boy's pet had been killed—obviously he had been careless in closing the lid of its tank. He ordered one of his team to comb Geneva in search of a pet shop which had a Mexican tarantula. Presumably all tarantulas looked the same, and with luck the boy wouldn't notice.

The phantom still lived, still scuttled, in Wanda's brain as she stood with her husband in the hall to receive their guests. Photographers poised. Then Grobichov was striding in with a beautiful blonde-haired young woman on his arm. Amazement and wonder seized everyone. Grobichov's dazzling smile and alertly gleaming eyes seemed not to notice it. 'Allow me to present my wife Larissa,' O'Reilly's interpreter murmured. Wanda's legs buckled; she gripped her husband's arm. Larissa, wearing a sable coat, held out a black-gloved hand. Hesitantly O'Reilly took it.

'You have two wives?'

Grobichov's double chin stretched back from his tight white collar and tie as he burst into a rich laugh. 'No, no! One is enough,' the interpreter translated solemnly.

Tremulously extending her hand to greet a black glove, Wanda said, 'Pardon me, I don't understand.' '*Izvinitye, ne ponimayu . . .*'

Cameras, as if recovering from their own astonishment, burst into activity, taking picture after picture, from all angles, of the radiantly beautiful Mrs Grobichov shaking hands with the stunned and suddenly geriatric First Lady. The peeling off of the sable revealed an off-the-shoulder black dress, and shoulders and breasts which might have been carved by a Renaissance master out of Carrara marble.

Hard-bitten journalists could not suppress their gasps. The no-news summit had exploded into life.

Grobichov's face became grave, concerned. 'I begin to see,' O'Reilly's awed interpreter echoed, 'there's been a stupid mis-understanding. The lady who was with me this afternoon is Larissa's mother. My wife felt unwell—she has a very bad cold, as I told you; Olga Ivanovna took her place.' He paused to let the translator catch up. 'We assumed you knew of this; one of my people telephoned. Or was supposed to. If it is our fault, I am very sorry. This is most embarrassing. Still, it is not serious.' He patted his wife's hand. 'Larissa is feeling better. All's well that ends well.'

· II ·

The dinner conversation struggled. It was bound to, with the four grey shadows having to translate every word. For, though Larissa Grobichov confessed to speaking English, having visited Great Britain with a Komsomol delegation some ten years ago, she did not choose to speak in a different tongue from her husband. In any case, she spoke very little, seeming in a sombre mood. She excused her dullness as an effect of her cold—two or three times she plucked a handkerchief from the sleeve of her elegantly simple black dress to wipe her nose.

Wanda was in shock, and also said little. O'Reilly, weary, kept missing what was said, and replied in a distracted manner. During the first two courses the liveliest remarks came from Grobichov—who was in the friendliest of moods—and, on one occasion, most unexpectedly, from Wanda's interpreter. Her contribution arose as a result of O'Reilly's mentioning the tentative trade agreements they had made in the little lakeside house. Grobichov asked how the IUD actually worked; Wanda, a blush mantling her rouge, said she wasn't sure; only that it was fitted into the womb and was very effective. He persisted, requested details. She couldn't give any.

It was at this point that Wanda's invisible shadow took on flesh, became an actual, quite attractive New York woman at whom they all stared, by murmuring: 'Pardon me, but I do know something about it—if it would help. I use it myself. It's a kind of zigzag shape, which is straightened out for insertion. It's not painful, especially if it's done during a period. Then it regains its shape in the womb. No one knows, quite, how it stops pregnancy. It may affect the lining of the womb, or prevent the fertilised egg from developing further. They've never really found out.'

She stopped, for Grobichov's shadow to interpret. He was nodding solemnly; his wife's face was bent over her plate. 'Thank you. It sounds like shamanistic magic,' observed the Russian leader with a smile. 'So this is the American technology you want to sell to me, Mr President! A piece of wire you don't understand!'

'But it works,' added the interpreter hurriedly, fearful that she'd wrecked a deal. 'It's worked for me and my—my significant other . . . *znachitel'ni drugoi*,' she explained for her hesitant Soviet counterpart. 'My lover. There are no side-effects. It's comfortable. I don't notice it.'

'How is it removed?' asked Grobichov, frowning.

'There's a little thread that hangs down through the cervix.'

'So'—his eyes sparkled— 'your great technological invention hangs by a little thread!'

The New Yorker, giving a frightened sideways glance at the First Lady, became a shadow, an insubstantial voice, once more.

When his favourite dessert, cherry pie and icecream, was served, the President became more animated. He cracked a joke; he spoke of his Texan ranch; of his grandson. Grobichov, too, had a grandson from his first marriage whom he loved. Here was something in common. The Russian had a photo of little Stiva in his wallet, and the boy was duly admired. Wanda, through tinted contact lenses, saw how coldly, indifferently, Larissa passed the photo across to her; and she could understand the second, as yet childless, wife having mixed feelings towards her husband's other life. Yet really there was no excusing the girl's sullen speechlessness. She was, frankly, dull; and Wanda began to feel that at least in the personality stakes there was no comparison. The press would realise this when they had to appear together at various functions the next day. Wanda cheered up a little, and promised to fetch some photos of their precious Tim.

'You know what he's gone and done?' chuckled O'Reilly. 'Invented a computer game called Shoot-Out!'

'And he's only six!' exclaimed Wanda.

'Is it a Western?' asked the bored Larissa.

'No, it's a war game. Some kind of science fiction rays in space fight it out with Sov—with nuclear weapons on earth! His father thinks it can be developed, put on the market. If it ever happens, we'll send one to your little Stiva.'

Larissa Grobichov said coldly, 'I think that's horrible. A child making a game out of nuclear weapons.'

'I agree,' said her husband.

'Do you?' O'Reilly stared into Larissa's blue eyes. His old heart flipped as her cold eyes held. And that slender waist, under her swelling breasts! That hint of steely hardness under her dress as his hand had guided her towards the dining-room! What a doll . . .

'Yes,' she said in English.

O'Reilly's eyes veered to Grobichov's. 'You too? I just thought your grandson . . . Oh, well . . . We'll send him something else.'

Grobichov's face relaxed, grew warmer again. 'That would be very nice. And we'll send your Tim a nice peaceful Russian present.'

That lifted the atmosphere. They would move into the

library for coffee. They rose—Grobichov dabbing his lips with
his napkin.

Wanda excused herself to get the photos. O'Reilly ushered
his guests ahead. Mako, Requiem and Bloomfield were in the
spacious library, before a roaring fire, drinking coffee.

'Don't get up,' Grobichov implored them, raising his hand.
They sank back.

'We're finished,' said Mako. 'We were just leaving. We have
a big session in the morning.'

'Oh, haven't you heard?' the Russian remarked, seating
himself by Mako on a sofa, reclining at ease, crossing his
pin-striped legs. 'There's no session. The President and I agreed
we do business better when we're on our own. You people are
too rancorous. I include my colleagues in that, too. We can all
have a long lie-in. The President and I will meet after lunch at
your chateau and sort things out by the fire.'

'Is this true, Mr President?'

'I meant to tell you guys.'

'I have to say I don't think this is wise,' said Requiem. Aghast,
the three negotiators craned forward. O'Reilly, perching on
a chair arm beside Larissa, ignored the remark. Wanda floated
in, in a haze of frills, carrying photos. Bloomfield stood, to
give her his chair. Before sitting, she glided to a stereo, and
clicked a switch. A Rachmaninov Concerto flooded the library:
she had thought of everything.

'Ah! *Chudno!* Isn't this like home, Larissa?'

'Wanda picked this out.'

'Lovely, yes.'

'And such a nice fire!'

'This is us on our ranch . . .'

'Do you take cream, Mrs Grobichov . . . ?'

And so, amidst the thunder of Russian music, the music of
a Russian in exile, the tension softened and the conversation
split among couples and trios.

'So this is the genius!' said Grobichov, with a sarcastic smile, as Wanda handed him a photo of Reuben Klein in tee-shirt and shorts, with his owlish son Tim.

'It was taken on our ranch at Christmas.'

Mako leaned over, trying to speak softly against the music. The Muscovite interpreter had difficulty catching the words. 'Yes, that's him. You've heard about it, I understand? The President's offered it to you?'

Grobichov frowned. 'How did you know that? I've told him I can't accept it. Nuclear missiles, defensive rays, shoot-outs in space—I think it's disgusting.'

Mako's face registered dismay. 'But I thought—'

Wanda, flushed, intervened. 'It was really just an idea we had, Walter.'

'It's much more than an idea.' Mako scowled at the First Lady. 'Comrade Grobichov, I assure you it's practicable and—'

Grobichov scowled. 'Mr Mako, I came to Geneva to talk about peace, to negotiate a nuclear reduction, not to talk about crazy, warmongering toys. Now if you'll excuse us . . .' He bent over a hastily produced polaroid of Tim and his mother swimming in the ranch pool.

Mako, flushed, rose and glided to where Requiem and the President huddled over the austere beauty, so shatteringly conjured out of thin air. After an exchange of pleasantries, the Secretary of State whispered in Requiem's ear: 'They're not taking the IUD.' He caught the eye of Bloomfield, browsing through the rows of mainly Hebrew books, and the arms expert glided up. 'You and I must talk, Jake.'

Announcing their goodnight, they shook Mrs Grobichov's slim warm hand, returned Grobichov's languid wave, and left. Requiem, unnoticed by the President, who was describing baseball to Larissa, got up from the chair arm and walked across to the other couple. He broke rudely into their picture session, saying, 'Pardon me, Mr Grobichov, but I'd like to have a quick word with you about the IUD.'

The glistening Russian eyes narrowed. 'I've already heard enough about it, Mr Requiem,' he growled. And Wanda protested, 'Please, Henry, no business tonight!'

'I came here to discuss nuclear arms reduction,' Grobichov growled.

'But I just wanted to say, you should consider it very seriously. It works.'

'But I'm told you don't know *how* it works.'

Requiem flinched. 'No, but that's only a matter of time,' he said.

The Russian waved a weary and dismissive hand. 'Look, I've told the President we'll consider it.'

'Oh!—you have?'

'Yes. And now, I'd really like to get to know this charming lady a little better.'

Wanda blushed.

'Oh—sure! Goodnight.'

Requiem walked out, saying goodnight to the President and his companion. They didn't notice.

'These damned technocrats!' growled Grobichov. 'Ours are just the same. I'd like to see round the house. It's very charming. Will you show me?'

'I'll be happy to.'

The sullen beauty was asked if she would like to come. No, she would rather nurse her cold by the fire and listen to the music. Would she like more coffee? *Nyet*. A brandy? *Nyet*. Wanda stood up. Her attendant shadow also rose.

Grobichov gabbled irately as his glance swept their efficient anonymous interpreters, four spectres at the feast. O'Reilly's translated without rancour: 'Listen: why don't we get rid of these idiots? They're a pain in the arse. I have to admit a white lie. I can speak a little English; perhaps just a little more English than

you speak Russian, Mr President. Larissa has been teaching me.'
Grobichov now spoke in almost fluent English: 'I was not sure if
I could follow you. Also, as you know, I'm new at this job; you're
very experienced and with a reputation for mental swiftness—
dancing like a butterfly, stinging like a bee, as your Mohammed
Ali says. I thought it would give me more time to gather my
thoughts if I waited for a translation. But you are very thoughtful, Mr President; you speak slowly, I find I can follow you. So
let's kick out these bums. No disrespect, you've done a fine job.'

He sat back, enjoying the effect of his revelation. The First
Lady sat again. 'Boy oh boy! You could knock me over with a
feather, Mr Grobichov! You speak beautiful English.'

'He's picked it up extremely fast,' said his wife, in an accent
that would not have disgraced the English home counties. 'I only
started coaching him a month ago, when the summit was arranged; and we've had to do it in odd half-hours here and there.'

'We don't need you guys.' O'Reilly clicked his fingers. The
four abashed interpreters glided from the library.

'Well, that's wonderful!' sighed Wanda. 'It's so much nicer
when you can understand each other. Look—I've been thinking
—can't we get away from this "Mr Grobichov" and "Mr
President" stuff? Can't you call us Wanda and Vince?'

'I'd be happy to.' Grobichov flashed a warm smile.

'Do we call you Alexei?'

'Alex will do.'

'Or Tiger,' said the President. 'I answer to both.'

'And it's Lar—?'

'Larissa,' said the blonde beauty, covering a yawn.

'That's a lovely name. For a lovely woman,' Wanda added
generously.

'So! Now we're really acquainted,' said Alex, rising, offering
Wanda his hand to help her up. 'Now show me this nice house,
Wanda.'

· 12 ·

Ten minutes later, in the President's bedroom, he was pressing Wanda to the wall, his mouth seeking hers and occasionally finding it. The sixty-year-old woman struggled feebly. She gasped 'No!' as his fingers massaged a scrawny breast; 'No, Alex!' as he pulled up her flouncy skirt at the front and started rubbing her well-defended genitals. He reached up to her waist, trying to insert his hand; but the combination of pantigirdle and pantihose defeated him. The effort seemed to weaken his desire; she was able to draw her lips away, panting, and push him off. He stood, gasping. Brushing her skirt down, she stepped past him to the bed and sat on it. 'Wow!' she said, and pressed her hand to her heaving bosom. 'Wow!'

He sat beside her, placed his hand on hers. 'I'm sorry,' he said. 'Please forgive me, Wanda!' He took from his pocket his silver cigarette case and lighter; lit a Sobranie. 'Your Californian wine must be stronger than I thought—but that doesn't excuse me.'

'Don't worry about it.'

'But I find you maddeningly attractive. I have done, ever

since we were introduced. People think we are not human. I'm only too human.'

'How can you find me attractive? Your wife is young and very beautiful.'

'Beauty isn't skin-shallow.'

'Skin-deep.'

'Ah yes! That was the phrase.'

Sighing, she took his hand in hers, turned it palm up, and kissed it. 'You're a very attractive man yourself.'

'Thank you.'

She glanced timidly at the closed door. 'I hope the security guard didn't hear anything.'

'I'm sure he didn't.'

'We have to be very careful, Alex. You know about the problems we've had. Well, of course you do.'

'Yes. I was genuinely sorry. Genuinely.'

She squeezed his hand. 'That's kind of you, Alex. You're a very nice man. I feel I can trust you, I don't know why.'

'You can.' He kissed her powdered cheek.

'It's been terrible. Mind you, I'm the one who's to blame. I was unfaithful, you see. Just a few times. With one of our drivers. Mr Johnson. Somehow, God knows how, Vince found out. It upset him so much, I guess he went a little crazy for a while. Oh, he's fine again now, but he started getting his own back on me, dragging up that old affair with the Fleming woman, and so on. It was terribly self-destructive, but he was hitting back at me, I guess.'

'I understand.'

'And this ex-driver made it worse by talking about it and exaggerating it. Luckily no one believed him, and poor Bill Shrub got blamed instead.'

'That's interesting,' said Grobichov, his brain making several lightning chess moves. 'Some of our people had a theory that Shrub was forced out because he was suspected of working for us. We knew your CIA thought Saltikov-Shchedrin was working for them. Absurd, of course! But we wondered if perhaps your people suspected Shrub of having warned us about him. Of course he didn't; but these secret service chiefs see moles everywhere.'

'Bill Shrub a mole?' she asked, incredulous. 'Well, I've never heard of such a thing! Bill's as straight as they come.'

'Well, of course he wasn't a mole!' Grobichov chuckled. 'And he seemed very pleasant, when we talked a while after Comrade Brezhenko's funeral.'

'He *is*. Dead straight. Vince tried to talk him out of resigning, after that misunderstanding arose in Klondyke's interview, but he insisted on going.'

Grobichov searched for an ashtray. There was none. Wanda offered him a porcelain bowl, which the absent owner's wife had cherished over many years. 'We ought to be getting back,' she said.

'Just a few minutes more, my dear,' he begged, his arm drawing her close. She sighed, and let him stroke her scrawny breasts. His mind was racing, writing an internal minute. O'Reilly had probably been foxing about Saltikov-Shchedrin. Well, now, when Wanda reported his words, he'd be worried about Shrub. They would have to reassess every secret decision and document to which Shrub had had access—which meant everything.

'This is what life is all about Wanda—not all that crap.'

'By the waters of Léman I sat down and wept.'

'A brandy would do your cold good. Sure you won't join me?'

'No. Thank you.'

'Why did you do that?'

'Why did I do what?'

Larissa had moved to a window, after her husband had gone out with Wanda; she had drawn back the curtain and stood gazing out at the dark waters of the lake. O'Reilly hovered behind her, a brandy balloon in hand.

He felt exhausted, felt every one of his seventy-five years dragging his body down to the earth. Yet the curves of this girl's back called to him; he longed to reach out a hand and touch her, longed to run his hand down the straight coils of her golden hair. He didn't dare to. More than four decades separated them.

O'Reilly could hardly remember the last time he had touched a woman amorously. Well, yes he could—just—it had to be that coloured bitch in New York who had turned him on by showing herself willing to have him tie her up. He'd got himself so worked up about her, he wrote that stupid letter. Then found, too late, she was a hooker and into blackmail.

But now, this Larissa—she seemed sad. Something was eating at her. He asked her what it was. Speaking to the window pane, she told him. It was to do with her husband's insensitivity. All that talk about IUDs, all that technology, when she, Larissa, had had a stillbirth only six months ago. Anyone but Alexei would have steered clear of the subject of wombs.

'I'm sorry,' he said, after the flood of confession was over. He lurched forward, and put an awkward arm round her waist. He thrilled again to the stiffness binding her flesh, under the smooth black dress. Letting his hand slide down over her hip and thigh, he thrilled to a hard contour at his fingertips in passing. Jesus, she *was* wearing garters. He'd suspected it when she'd sat sipping coffee—the hint of a garter-button breaking her skirt's smooth line—but O'Reilly had ascribed it to his imagination. Like those fucking pin-up pictures of Wanda, forty years back. His head spun, picturing the creamy thighs bursting out of strap-tugged nylon. No—silk.

She turned to him. The lashes under her clear-blue eyes were wet. 'I shouldn't be telling you this,' she said, gliding past, moving back to her armchair. She sat down and crossed her long and shapely, black-veiled legs. O'Reilly took the sofa, opposite. No, her dress was too long to see anything; but his hand, cradling the brandy balloon, trembled as he stared at the long, spiky heel of an elegant black shoe. She leaned back, closing her eyes. 'No man can understand what it feels like,' she murmured, 'to give birth to a baby you know to be dead, and then hold it in your arms. I don't expect Alexei to understand. But his questions this evening were beyond anything.'

'Wanda had a miscarriage once. I understand how you must feel.'

'But even a miscarriage is not quite the same. My baby was perfect. They never found out why she died.'

'It must have been awful, Larissa.' O'Reilly bent low, pretending to pick up a carelessly discarded mint paper, but still couldn't get a glimpse of white above the hose. He straightened, grunting.

'Perhaps it was a punishment on me,' she went on, sighing.

'Really?'

'Yes.'

'A punishment for what?'

'Oh, for bad things I did, before I met Alexei.' She opened her eyes wide, and stared at the wall past his shoulder, as if at some unspeakable horror. 'I had an affair with an older man—older even than Alexei. He used to do dreadful things to me—tie me up and hit me, or get his friends to screw me. And I let him do it, I even got kind of hooked on it. I suppose I'm drawn to powerful older men!'

'Well, we've all done things we regret.'

'*Pravda*. That's true.'

As Larissa's confession slowly penetrated damaged neurons, O'Reilly shivered.

'Yes,' she said, pulling herself up in the chair and smoothing her dress over her knees, 'there is a lot I regret. I don't suppose I should blame Alexei, because I'm sure I should find a kind, sensitive man boring. All the same, he should have sensed he was touching a very painful nerve. Not that your people helped.' She turned her gaze full on O'Reilly. 'What's so important about these contraceptives? Why do you want to unload them on to us?'

'That's fortunate for Alex,' said the President, his voice slightly shaky. 'He's very powerful. And older—although he doesn't seem old to me. He's young enough to be my son. Damn him, I envy him, Larissa!' He twisted his large mouth into a grin.

She persisted, trying to draw an answer out. 'Do you want our population growth to decline?' She smiled lightly.

'No particular reason. It's a humanitarian gesture. We know a lot of abortions go on in your country, and we'd like to prevent some of them.'

She shrugged.

'Not if it would cut off the supply of beautiful girls! I love your dress, by the way. Did you get it in Moscow?'

She flicked the black silk. 'No, here. Somebody bought it for me this morning. The days of shopping on my own are gone, I'm afraid.'

They heard voices, and the door opened. Wanda entered, followed by Grobichov.

'It's a beautiful house, Larissa.'

'Well, it suits you,' said O'Reilly.

The Russian leader rocked back on his heels, but smiled in amusement. 'Unfortunately I don't have any well-heeled Jewish friends,' he said. 'I have to make do with our stuffy Mission.'

· 13 ·

'Talking of our Jewish friends,' said Wanda, 'their staff have made some kind of special cake for us, and I've asked them to bring it in, just before you have to go. They're dying to see you. Is that okay?'

Grobichov, flinging himself into a chair near his wife, nodded. Wanda picked up the phone and said, 'Tell them they can bring the cake in now.' She sat by her husband on the sofa; patted his hand. 'Did you two have a nice chat, dear?'

'They've had to put up with a lot,' he said. 'All the security checks, having the house turned upside down, that kind of thing. They'll appreciate meeting you. Yes, Larissa and I got along real swell.'

'That's good,' said Grobichov. 'So did we. I'll tell you something—we're finding that we're all human. You had us down as devils, and we had you down as sharks. Mako, Requiem, Tiger—all breedings of sharks!'

'Breeds,' Larissa corrected.

'Breeds. Thanks. We looked up sharks in an encyclopedia and found you were shark-men from Hawaii—*mano tanaka*, sharks who swim ashore and turn into men! That's how we had you figured!'

He chuckled, and dabbed his balding head with a handkerchief. There was a timid knock at the door. Wanda called, 'Come in.' A white-coated servant backed in, pulling a trolley. After him came a string of self-conscious, awed servants, from butler to housemaid—nearly a dozen in all, evenly divided between male and female, pale-faced Swiss and burnished Semites. The last one in, the chef (he was wearing his hat) closed the door gently. The trolley and its contents came to rest in the middle of the library, between the relaxing couples. 'My!' Wanda exclaimed. 'Isn't that just something!'

'*Chudno!*' agreed Grobichov.

Abashed, pleased, the members of Hymie Weinstock's staff hung their heads and stood awkwardly. Their creation was indeed *chudno,* was indeed just something: a cake in the shape of a globe, the earth, with its seas and continents depicted by different coloured icing. It was studded with tiny flags of all the various countries. And it was crowned, at the North Pole, with a white dove, its iced wings poised for flight.

O'Reilly said, 'We want to thank you people for   ' But there was a sudden flurry of silent movement; three of the Semitic-looking servants had pistols in their hands, two of which were pressed to the temples of O'Reilly and Wanda. The chef locked the door; his pistol covered the rest of the astonished gathering. A scullery maid screamed. 'Against the wall!' snarled the chef, waving his gun at the servants. 'Move! Hands above your heads!' The terrified servants did as they were told, fleeing to the wall and lifting their hands, as if in prayer to the benevolent portrait of their employer, Hymie Weinstock. A security guard was hammering at the door and shouting.

'You! O'Reilly!' hissed the chambermaid whose pistol barrel nudged the President's skull. 'Tell him you're a dead man if they try to interfere.'

'What the fuck are you guys—?'

'Tell him!'

O'Reilly shouted shakily: 'There's been a hold-up. They'll shoot us if you try anything.'

The hammering and shouting stopped.

'That's better,' said the olive-skinned, burning-eyed chambermaid. 'You all ought to know the cake is a bomb. One false move from anyone and we all go up.'

Wanda shuddered; her eyes closed. At her side the wine waiter, who had poured the Californian wines so adroitly and courteously, scraped the barrel against her brow.

Larissa Grobichov, white-faced, sat tensed on the edge of her chair. Her husband still sprawled back nonchalantly. 'Who are you people?' he demanded.

'Never you mind,' snapped the chef. 'Just sit still and you won't get hurt.'

'Are you Palestinians?'

'Shut up.'

'O'Reilly,' hissed the chambermaid, 'we want you to lift the phone and order your helicopter. And have them fuel your plane ready for take-off. If the helicopter isn't here within thirty minutes, your wife gets shot. Tell them that.' Wanda, at O'Reilly's side, gave a gasp and fainted. Larissa rose from her seat but the chef waved her back.

'Get up!' ordered the chambermaid, prodding O'Reilly with the gun. He rose and sleepwalked to the phone, with the young terrorist shadowing him. 'Make it clear to them they're not to try anything. It won't bother us in the least to shoot you both. You're both Jew–loving imperialist scum. It would give me great pleasure to blow a hole in your head. Tell it to them good.'

O'Reilly lifted the phone and spoke down it somnambulistically. He shuffled back to his prostrate wife.

'May I smoke?' asked Grobichov, indicating the silver cigarette case he had been opening when the hi-jack began. Taking silence as assent, he selected a Sobranie and lit up. He breathed in deeply.

'What was that?' snapped the chef, glancing at the curtained window. His companions shifted their gaze; the chef's pistol fired twice; the chambermaid and the wine waiter slid to the floor. Screams filled the library; the shouts and hammerings started again outside. 'Quiet!' roared the hook-nosed chef, and the bedlam stopped. Backing to the door, he called, 'It's all right! The terrorists are dead! Everyone's safe!'

Larissa was being consoled in Grobichov's arms; cigarette smoke seemed to be curling from her shoulder. Two tearful Swiss servants were helping the President bring Wanda round.

The chef approached the Russian couple. 'Mossad?' asked Grobichov. The young man shrugged. Solicitously he removed Larissa from her husband's embrace, then pressed his pistol to her brow. 'Okay, it's not yet over!' he shouted. Everyone looked in their direction; gasped. 'The bomb is still primed. Mr President, I'm sorry. Just stay out of this and you'll soon be free.'

'What do you want?' asked Grobichov, his eyes narrowed, his finger tapping off ash into a heavy glass ashtray.

Keeping his pistol trained on the swaying white-faced beauty, the chef fumbled in a pocket of his white coat and produced a folded-up sheet of paper. He gave it to the Soviet leader, who unfolded and scanned it. He frowned.

'You must ring the Kremlin and read out those names. They must be put on a plane for Geneva and arrive here before noon tomorrow. If they don't, I'll shoot your wife.'

Dragging on his cigarette, Grobichov reflected. 'Impossible,' he growled. 'These are obviously criminals and lunatics. I know some of them all too well. We can't let them go.'

'It's your choice.' Clutching Larissa from behind, he caressed her delicate ear with the gun barrel.

'In any case, they are scattered all over the Soviet Union. It would be impossible to fly them here so quickly.'

'By noon tomorrow. Also you will issue an order, to be broadcast every hour throughout Russia, to the effect that all Jews who wish to emigrate to the West, now or at any time in the future, will be allowed to leave.'

Narrowed, glittering eyes and an uptilted black Sobranie confronted the Jewish terrorist aggressively. Instead of inhaling, Grobichov blew, like blowing dandelion seeds, at the Zionist's throat. His eyes widened; something that looked like a minute splinter had stuck in his skin. The young man seemed to freeze for a moment, then—his arm sliding down Larissa's dress—he fell to the floor. Grobichov spat out the cigarette and caught hold of his wife. A servant rushed to the door, as pandemonium broke out again, and released the lock. The door burst open; security guards, weapons at the ready, charged in and rushed to the President. A soldier, eyeing the global cake, ordered everyone out of the room. 'What the hell happened to this guy?' asked the guard, kneeling by the dead Zionist.

The Russian leader pointed to his cigarette case. 'A touch of James Bond,' he explained. 'I have to take care not to smoke the ones at the end. It works instantly. No time to pull the trigger. And anyway, darling,' he said to his wife in Russian, stroking her hair, 'the safety catch was on—you were in no danger. He was an amateur.' His polished shoe scuffed the corpse.

'They were taken on the staff here about six weeks ago,' said a dressing-gowned, sick-looking Mako. 'All three together. Probably they were planning to kidnap Weinstock or his family. The summit was just a stroke of unbelievable good luck for them. Or would have been. If Mossad hadn't infiltrated their cell. We weren't informed. I guess because this guy and whoever operated him were rogues, working for themselves.'

Mako, Requiem, the exhausted President and the Soviet

couple sat hunched over coffee and cognac in a small lounge. The house had quietened. The presidential helicopter had landed, as instructed, and whirred off again. The cake had been defused.

'How do I know your people didn't set this up?' growled Grobichov.

'And risk the President's life?'

Grobichov shrugged. 'I suppose so. Yes, I must trust you.'

'You were wonderfully brave, sir,' admitted Requiem.

'Well, it's good I didn't have to rely on your security. It was appalling.'

'Yes, we owe you a debt of thanks, Alec,' said the President tiredly.

The Russian's frown softened. 'All's well that ends well. I'm glad I lit up. I was thinking, if your guards burst in when the President was being threatened, I could have taken one of them out. The hi-jackers, I mean.'

'They're some cigarettes!' chuckled Mako.

Grobichov seized his wife's hand and squeezed it. She smiled at him wanly. 'You're tired, *golubchik*. We must go. Tomorrow, the show must go on. You agree?'

Mako and Requiem murmured assent. They looked at the President. His hand held his coffee cup in mid-air, yet his eyes were shut and he was breathing nasally. Mako took the cup from his hand and set it down. 'The President's bushed.'

'I hope Mrs O'Reilly will feel better in the morning.'

'I'm sure she will. A good night's rest. And *you* get a good night's sleep, Mrs Grobichov.' Mako patted her knee.

'I will.' She smiled palely. 'I'm okay.'

'I can't get over how well you guys speak English. One important thing—can I take it this little affair hasn't happened?'

Grobichov nodded. 'We've had a very nice dinner.'

'Good. We'll handle the servants. It all went very well. They baked you a nice cake with a dove on it.'

· 14 ·

Clipping on the diamond earrings which served her also as a delicate concealed hearing aid, Wanda O'Reilly suddenly felt she couldn't go through with the day's programme. She gazed in the mirror at the President's bolstered and pyjama'd reflection, and said, 'I just can't go through with it, honey.'

O'Reilly, occasionally rumbling with chuckles, was turning the pages of the *Digest*. Rouged and mascara'd, yet unmistakably 'wrinkled deep in time' after the horrors of the previous day, she swivelled on her seat to confront him.

'This is a nice article on Bergman—did you read it?'

'No. Is it very cowardly of me?'

'Can't go through with what?'

'The coffee date with Mrs Grobichov. The press conference with her at the children's home. I can't do it.'

'No, you've gone through a lot.' He turned a page; nudged his reading glasses back along his nose.

The beauty and the beast, Larissa and tarantula, and the cold steel of the pistol, mixed into one horrific image in Wanda's mind and made her feel faint again. Roused from drugged sleep by Katie's phone call, she had read between the lines of her daughter's tact that all Washington—probably the whole world—was rocking with laughter over her, Wanda's, discomfiture. The TV stations would be playing, over and over, and one after the other, her hand-shakes with the Grobichov consorts.

'They'll be waiting to see how I react,' she said; 'comparing our complexion, our hairstyles, our clothes—ready to take me apart. But they're not going to! Oh, no! They can go fuck themselves.' She began peeling off her gold lamé pants-suit.

'I'll tell Mako to call them,' said O'Reilly.

She slipped into a white wrap, tied it, and flopped out on her bed. 'Oh, I meant to tell you,' she said, after resting a while, 'while I was showing Alex around, he said something kind of strange about Bill Shrub. Something about wondering if you suspected he was a Soviet mole, Tiger.'

'It mentions us here, at that charity show in LA with Ingrid.'

'This could be important. You don't think Bill could have been involved in anything tricky?'

O'Reilly laid the magazine on the quilt and stared thoughtfully into space. 'That's interesting. I had a gut feeling it was Shrub who'd betrayed our mole, when he resigned so quietly. Well, that's good—he never got a sight of anything important.'

He picked up the *Digest*, but a blue-covered document on the bedside table caught his eye. With a sigh, he tossed the magazine aside and picked up the document. It was Requiem's memorandum on the ever-increasing superiority of the Soviets in nuclear armaments, thousands of copies of which were circulating in Geneva. Henry kept asking him if he'd read it yet, and the Tiger kept stalling. He'd have to glance at the damned thing. It was full of incomprehensible facts and figures. O'Reilly groaned. A President's job was never done.

Reporters and photographers turned away from the Soviet Mission. There were to be no coffee pictures, since the First Lady had an upset stomach. More sensationally, there were no round table negotiations going on: the President and Mr Grobichov had found their by-now-famous 'walk in the woods' so refreshing and useful that they had decided to take the negotiations into their own hands. The press centre was buzzing; myriad languages jostled through the telephone wires. This was hot news: perhaps the first hint of constructive dialogue, or at the very least that the two men felt they could talk to each other.

The only negotiations were between pressmen. Who would cover the second walk through the woods, scheduled for two o'clock? Who would cover the programmed—but now doubtful—meeting of the first ladies at a Geneva children's home, at the same hour? The Russians had guaranteed Larissa Grobichov's presence, even if Wanda O'Reilly was still too unwell to join her, and she would be happy to answer questions.

It was a tricky decision. At the Chateau Belle de Nuit, they might catch only a tantalising glimpse of the world leaders, flitting between trees. The pressmen were slavering to get a close look at the phantom of beauty who had suddenly appeared at Grobichov's side. Was she as intelligent as she was lovely, or were her brains in her tits? Even if the high drama of a Wanda–Larissa contest was to be denied them, the pressmen, western and eastern, knew where they wanted to be—staring down Larissa's cleavage. Yet, in so doing, they might just conceivably miss some moment of high political drama at the chateau.

What bums, to schedule both events at the same time! So they debated, within and among themselves, and argued, and negotiated.

The Tiger hunched over a working lunch with his team. Between bites at a triple-decker salad sandwich, Mako outlined what they believed the President's negotiating stance should be. He should do everything in his power to persuade Grobichov to agree the IUD deal. He had not, it was clear, quite closed the door on it. True, to Mako he'd sounded off about American aggression, nuclear toys, that kind of stuff; but Requiem had goaded him into an admission that they were still considering the deal. 'Isn't that right, Henry?' Mako concluded, flashing a glance left.

Requiem came out of a daze. For once, he hadn't been following closely. In truth, he had spent a sleepless night: anguished by the failure of the brilliant scheme he had cooked up with Mossad, the Israeli intelligence agency. Grobichov's damned James Bond gadgetry had screwed up what could have been the collapse of the summit and a gigantic *coup* for America and freedom.

He was forced to say, 'I'm sorry, my mind was somewhere else. Isn't what right?'

'Wake up, Henry!' Mako dribbled tomato juice and pips. 'They're still considering IUD.'

'That's right, Mr President. He told me so.'

'So obviously,' said Mako, dabbing his chin with a stiff napkin, 'they're telling us there's a price. Well, that's not surprising. It's amazing they're considering it at all, since there's really nothing in it for them.'

O'Reilly, biting into a hamburger, frowned. 'The guy's agreed to take the IUD in principle. I've no reason to think he'll backtrack on it, if the price is reasonable.'

'Oh?' said Mako. 'I got the idea, from something Wanda said, that he'd brought it up again over dinner and turned it down flat. Grobichov got very angry and Wanda kind of said, Well, it was only an idea, and gave me a warning-off look. You didn't discuss it over dinner?'

'Oh, I wouldn't say that.'

'Well, anyway, you can take my word for it, it's touch and go. I've been talking to the Pentagon. Talking to people in the House. As a matter of fact, I've only had a couple of hours' sleep. Everyone's pretty damn excited about the idea; but the consensus is, there'll be a lot of opposition. It's bound to take years of research and cost a lot of money. Also, it looks aggressive rather than defensive.'

Requiem smiled, before burying his nose in a yoghourt carton.

'It came up, yes. He wanted to know how it works.'

'Well, of course.'

'That's what he said to me,' murmured Requiem through yoghourt-stained lips. 'That we don't even know how it works yet.'

'Research . . . money . . .' grunted the President. 'That's not our problem. They'll pay for what we've got. Who cares how it works as long as it works.'

Mako caressed his coffee cup thoughtfully. 'The point is, they obviously want us to move on Europe. And Henry and I agree we should do that. If, by some miracle, they agree to take the IUD, we shan't have any problems back home—or among our allies. The public will love it.'

'Wanda's interpreter was a great help on that,' O'Reilly murmured. 'We learned a great deal from her. She seemed a bright kid.'

'Fine. But there's really no doubt about it; the man in the street will just love it. Collaboration with the Russians. So it's important enough to give them something on Europe, Tiger. Say, fifty per cent reduction in our Cruises and Pershings, for a corresponding reduction in SS-20s on European soil.'

Requiem nodded. 'It won't really matter. The IUD will give us an overwhelming advantage.'

Mako nodded. 'It'll still be a miracle if they agree. But we can only try.'

O'Reilly nodded. 'I'll do that. You really think an IUD deal would be *that* good for us, Henry?'

Requiem and Mako grinned at the joke. O'Reilly smiled happily and said he was looking forward to the fireside chat. 'Oh, by the way, Henry: I'd like you to cover for Wanda at the kids' home.' He rose from the table; Requiem looked taken aback by the request: what if the President needed his advice? The President strode to the door. Requiem sprang in pursuit. A junior aide, licking his lips nervously, intercepted the President outside: 'Oh, Mr President, we can't get hold of a tarantula.'

'Then I'll just have to fall back on Walter,' said the President drily.

Relieved by O'Reilly's humour, the boyish aide chuckled; then explained earnestly: 'We've tried every pet-shop in Geneva. They don't seem to go for them here.'

The President exploded: 'What do you mean, you can't get hold of one? Look harder, damn you! Do I have to do every fucking thing myself? Do you expect me to negotiate with Russia and also find a replacement tarantula?'

'No, sir.'

'Call Vienna—Paris—London. Mexico City, if necessary. That kid's put his trust in me. Get them to fly one here, damn it!'

'Yes, sir.'

15

One corner of the assembly hall of the Pestalozzi School for Battered Children had been arranged to look like a nursery classroom. There were small tables and chairs, a blackboard, and a wall-display of childish paintings. The corner was empty; no children were present. Which was perhaps just as well, since the rest of the hall was packed with members of the press—at least two hundred of them. They broke into clapping as Henry Requiem, US Defence Secretary, appeared from behind a stage-curtain, closely followed by Larissa Grobichov and two interpreters.

Fashion reporters in the audience immediately noted that Mrs Grobichov was rather dowdily dressed, in a white high-necked sweater, grey pleated skirt and calf-length boots. The males, in contrast, didn't seem aware of this; the one or two vulgar wolf-whistles brashly conveyed the reaction of all the assembled, hard-bitten news-hounds. Her fine-spun long straight blonde hair sparkled in a flash of wintry sunlight through the broad window; her large blue eyes seemed to reach and caress the final males crowded at the door; her smile was friendly and generous. The first pictures hadn't lied: she was a bombshell.

She and the two shadowy interpreters seated themselves. Requiem, an altogether less charismatic figure in his black three-piece suit and rimless specs, stood before a microphone, frowning at the crude whistles. He announced, with heavy humour, that they'd have noticed he wasn't the First Lady. He brought, however, her apologies and good wishes to the school. As they knew, she had a slight stomach-upset; nothing serious. He was very happy to introduce Mrs Grobichov to them, and wouldn't take up much of their time. But they would probably like to know that the negotiations so far had been useful and businesslike. The President and Mr Grobichov found they could talk to each other. The atmosphere had at times been very frank, but there was no table thumping from the Soviet side; Mr Grobichov was no Khrushchev. And now he would hand them over to Mrs Grobichov, if they had any questions to put to her.

But they weren't going to let him get away so easily. Several reporters jumped up, and Requiem, poised to sit down, turned again to face them.

'Mr Secretary, has there been any kind of breakthrough on the disarmament question?'

'You know I can't talk about the negotiations. You'll get a statement tomorrow.'

'But do you expect any positive agreements to be announced?'

'We've always said we don't anticipate any miracles at this summit.'

'Are the rest of you happy that the two leaders seem to have taken the negotiations into their own hands?'

'Quite happy. The rest of us, on both sides, aren't exactly having a winter vacation, you know!' He smiled bleakly, his spectacles flashing.

'Can you tell us why the President's helicopter landed on the lawn of his villa last night, and then took off again almost immediately?'

'It was just routine security.'

'So the report that Stanislav Finn was called in to help smooth a tricky atmosphere isn't true?'

There was a stir among the news men. Geneva had been buzzing with the rumour: Finn, the UN chief negotiator, had been whirled from his Geneva headquarters to prevent the summit breaking up in a cloud of bitter recrimination.

'It's not true. No more questions. Mrs Grobichov?' He turned with a smile. She rose, along with the English-speaking interpreter; Requiem and the Russian interpreter sat down. Larissa began by saying how pleased she was to be here at the school, since education was dear to her heart and the hearts of all Soviet citizens. She looked forward to meeting the children. She had hoped to have Mrs O'Reilly alongside her, but wished her a speedy recovery. She would be glad to answer any questions.

They came thick and fast. Laughing, she had to appeal for patience and order. Also, they should please consider the poor interpreter; for, though she herself had some English, not every Soviet journalist in the room was in that position, so she would speak in her native tongue. She then answered each question fully, with smiles, with humour, with the skill of a practised lecturer in Marxist-Leninist psychology. Where she had met her husband; the similarities and differences of their natures; the problems of combining a responsible job with fulfilling her new duties; her first reactions (agreeable) to the President and Mrs O'Reilly: all were handled tactfully and—even if her clothes were dowdy—with a designer style.

Her smile and charm froze up a little only when she was taxed, as a psychologist, with the Soviet abuse of psychiatry in the punishment of dissidents. The tones of her warm Russian speech became noticeably cooler. The attitude to mental illness in the two countries was different. They believed that if patients felt they could serve society and be useful, they were more likely to get better. 'Mental illness fundamentally is feeling useless, unneeded,' she said. So, naturally, there was an emphasis on social rehabilitation. There were no dissidents in mental hospitals who were not genuinely sick; that was to say, alienated from normality, healthy social values. Why, Stanislav Finn, whose name had been brought up, had himself investigated the Soviet psychiatric hospitals and given them a clean bill of health.

She stopped; her smile stole back; the English-speaking interpreter dabbed his brow. The tension in the audience eased as she dealt gracefully with more light-hearted questions, beginning with one from a Soviet journalist.

'Could you tell us about your mother? Why did she come with you?'

'Ah! My mother is a wonderful woman. I owe everything to her. She has worked very hard. My father is a coal miner, so of course he would always come home very tired, and it was mother who really talked to her children and told us stories. Incidentally, I should tell you that my father earns as much as me! Truly! In the Soviet Union you are paid according to your desserts. But my mother, she is warm and wonderful. She has never been abroad, and she hardly ever has a break, so it seemed like a good idea to have her along.'

Whose idea had it been, an American asked, for her mother to take her place at the opening? The question brought chuckles round the hall.

'My husband's.'

'Was it a propaganda ploy?'

The chuckles spread, and Larissa's smile widened. 'Not in the least! It was an unfortunate mistake that the information didn't get through to the chateau; and then the introductions were hurried, in the cold wind. So the unfortunate mix-up occurred.' She plucked a tissue from her sleeve and blew her nose. 'I was very unhappy to miss the opening, but I felt just too unwell to make it—like Mrs O'Reilly today.'

'That suggests, Mrs Grobichov, you think her sick stomach may be a tit-for-tat?'

The chuckles were open and universal; but Mrs Grobichov kept a straight face. '*Nyet.*'

'Who do you feel won out on the dress front last night—you or Wanda O'Reilly?'

She shook her head impatiently. 'I've no idea. It's stupid. There are far more important questions to be tackled here in Geneva.'

'Do you take an interest in politics? I mean, apart from your role as Comrade Grobichov's wife?'

'Oh yes, of course, like every responsible Soviet citizen. I've tried to follow the disarmament issue carefully, and to understand it. I've read a lot of commentaries on it, both Russian and American.'

'American?'

'Yes. I've read Witmann, Schlesinger . . . But I find it hard going. I would rather read poetry—Pushkin, Lermontov, Akhmatova, Mayakovsky, for instance. They are the best preparation for a summit, better than the political polemicists, I think.'

A reporter waved a blue document. 'Have you read Requiem?' He smiled sardonically; eyes glanced at the impassive Secretary for Defence.

'Of course. Our reading is not so narrow!'

'What do you think of it?'

'I think it's very moving.'

A rustle of incredulity swept the audience. 'Moving' was the last word one would choose to describe Requiem's turgid, fanatical monograph. Even the author looked embarrassed, shuffling his knees.

'But it's very one-sided and obsessional,' she continued evenly. 'You won't find a rounded, truthful picture of my country in *Requiem*. What you do find is power, majestic utterance, combined with supreme simplicity . . .' Again a subdued tumult of disbelief swept through the hall. 'Oh yes! how can one not admire *Requiem*? But don't look for balance. You could say, of course, that *Requiem* is too short to be balanced.'

The babble of her English translator was succeeded by an outcry of hilarity and disbelief. Pandemonium broke out. Mrs Grobichov looked bewildered. Brick-red, the somewhat undersized Requiem stood up and stalked from the stage.

A Soviet journalist, who from case endings and other hints had well understood Larissa's reference, and who was baffled and annoyed by the barrage of noise around him, shouted for silence. Gradually, a reasonable decorum was restored. With angry sympathy he spoke his question:

'Comrade Grobichova, wouldn't you agree Mayakovsky is the better poet?'

More hilarity broke out. Requiem wasn't *any* kind of poet! He wouldn't know a poem from a piss-pot.

'I agree.'

'But in any case there are better works by Akhmatova than *Requiem*. Wouldn't you say?'

'Of course. Her patriotic poems in the war, for example. But here in the West they only know this one work, *Requiem*.'

The noise became stilled. Puzzlement had passed from Soviet to American faces. Larissa Grobichov wore a light smile. Then she talked enthusiastically of Pushkin and Tolstoy and Gorky, lamenting the barrier of language which prevented the poets and writers of all races from coming together and performing in harmony. Now *that* would be a summit! With every journalist in the hall silent and eating out of her hand, she brought the press conference to an end.

The reporters fought to get out; the photographers lingered. After the hall was cleared of the former, a young female teacher led in a line of fearful, uncomprehending little boys and girls, and got them to sit round the tables in the corner. Then Mrs Grobichov stepped down from the stage and walked towards the children, smiling warmly. She shook hands with the teacher, then squatted to address the children in French. She promised to send, to every child in the home, a Russian doll. Thumbs in their mouths, the children didn't reply, but stared at the mysterious lady. The photographers crowded round; cameras flashed. When the five minutes allowed was up, Larissa kissed a little boy on the forehead, and stood up. One of the Soviet journalists, who had asked a question, had lingered near the group. Uncertainly he approached her. 'Comrade Grobichova, excuse me: I'm very happy to meet you. One or two of our photographers and I thought of taking some of the children out for a walk; perhaps buy them a nice tea. Do you think that would be a good idea?'

'I think that would be splendid!' she said. 'We'll ask their teacher.'

'Good! Thank you!'

He patted the head of a bright-looking, attractive little boy, who gazed up at him rapturously.

'Your face is slightly familiar,' said Larissa. 'You are—?'

'Spassky. I edit *Cement*.'

16

Their hands were intertwined and firm; their eyes and mouths poured forth affection; sunlight sparkled off Grobichov's bald skull and O'Reilly's red locks. The joined hands pumped, held still, and pumped again. Side by side, overcoated, the leaders set off down the woodland path and the cameramen trooped inside for a drink.

Branches crackled underfoot, the wind off the lake stung the leaders' amicable faces. Grobichov hoped Wanda was feeling better? Yes, her stomach had settled, a little, and she would surely be well enough to dine tonight at the Soviet Mission. Ah, that was good! exclaimed Grobichov. He liked her. And the feeling was mutual, said the President. *He* had really enjoyed making Larissa's acquaintance.

The President's hand caught at a firm, taut birch trunk, and he thought of Larissa's firmly controlled body. He shivered, and Grobichov said, 'Yes, it's gone colder. I hope there's a nice fire blazing?'

And there was. As they entered the lakeside house, they were greeted by warmth and the bitter-sweet scent of the crackling logs. A coffee percolator bubbled; a bottle of champagne peeped from a silver bucket of ice.

'That's for if we have anything to celebrate, Alex,' said the President, removing his overcoat. He sank into a fireside chair. Grobichov, doffing his coat also and settling at the other side of the hearth, within touching distance, exclaimed, 'We must make sure that we have!'

O'Reilly spoke about the American Dream. About Abraham Lincoln starting life in a log cabin; about his own poor background, his father a loving but feckless Irish bricklayer. Grobichov listened politely: lighting up a Sobranie—carefully avoiding the ones at either end. When O'Reilly paused in his dissertation on American values, the Russian countered by describing his own humble origins. His plump face ruddy in the fire-glow, he spoke with sad-sweet *toská* of his early years as a coal miner in the Urals; of his first wife helping him to wash the grime off after a long, hard shift.

'You know, Vince,' he said, with a heavy sigh, 'sometimes I wish I was right back there. You and I carry a terrible burden. Either one of us could blow up the world a hundred times over. And you know what?' Stretching forward, he touched O'Reilly's knee. 'Power is hard to give up. It's always natural to want more of anything, not less. There's a little demon in me which wants my country to be stronger than it was under Brezhenko. Do you understand me?'

'I know how you feel. The days when you're struggling to rise are the best.'

'Precisely! But for the sake of the world, Vince, we've got to start trusting each other, and stripping ourselves of power. Let me tell you a Russian fairy tale. About the Firebird, which is half-beast and half-angel. She had beautiful, magical feathers. They were the source of her strength. One day a sorcerer in the shape of a giant raven seized her and whirled her up into the sky. For the sake of the earth she was leaving behind, the

Firebird started shedding her glowing feathers. They fluttered down to earth, and were soon covered by grass and leaves. But they still glow brilliantly, and give life. The poor Firebird, however, was losing all her strength, and knew she must die. Yet she still went on shedding her feathers, for the sake of humanity.' Grobichov paused, his beady eyes staring queryingly into O'Reilly's.

'I understand.'

Grobichov nodded. 'We must strip ourselves of our power, like the Firebird, Vince. Our power lies, God help us, in our missiles. We must cast them off, we must become weak.'

'That's a beautiful story,' said the President. 'I can see what you're getting at.'

'I beg you, I plead with you, Mr President—Vince—to trust us! And I hope we can trust you. This is perhaps the most important hour of our life.' He waved his arms excitedly. 'Let's make generosity and trust our watchwords! Let's make this the Firebird summit, as well as the fireside summit, my friend!'

'You mean we should drop our missiles?'

Grobichov looked horrified; then understanding dawned. 'Yes, drop them, get rid of them, destroy them. Give, give, give to each other! Out-do each other in trust and generosity, my friend!'

O'Reilly nodded. That was how he felt too. The Firebird summit.

'These are no mere words I am speaking,' said the Russian leader. His fist hammered the arm of his chair. 'I mean them, with every bone in my body . . . There's one thing, Mr President—Tiger—before we go any further. Can I take it you have full authority to negotiate here this afternoon for your country?'

O'Reilly, moved by the Russian's sincerity, nodded emphatically.

'The threat to impeach you is over?' asked Grobichov.

'Yes.'

Grobichov relaxed; sighed. 'That's good. So we can trust, and be generous . . . for the sake of peace.'

O'Reilly nodded; gulped coffee.

'I'm still not sure you really believe me,' complained Grobichov, leaning forward, touching the President's knee. 'About trust and generosity. For instance—you admire my wife. Do you want her?'

O'Reilly nodded; his eyes glazed; he was damned tired after all those speeches.

'Well, it's possible. She likes older, powerful men. In my ancestral tribe, from Lake Baikal, it was the custom to offer one's wife to a guest for the night. And tonight you'll come to us . . . We'll wait and see. I make no commitments! This is not negotiable!' His eyes sparkled. He took his hand from O'Reilly's knee, and sank back, drawing in on the black cigarette.

The President made a choking noise; his powerful, trunklike body shivered. 'Is my smoke bothering you?' asked Grobichov.

'No. No.'

'Then let's get down to real business. Pull back your Cruise and Pershing missiles from Europe, and we'll pull back our SS- 20s. Now, what do you say? In trust and generosity. Is it such a bad deal for you?'

'No, please carry on.'

'I've said what I have to say.'

'Make it fifty per cent on each side, and we could be in business.'

Grobichov's fingers shook. He could hardly believe his ears. But he contrived to look slightly disappointed. He suggested fifty per cent now, the rest in two years' time. O'Reilly hummed, hesitated, finally said, 'Okay—but on one condition.'

The Russian tensed. 'And what's that?'

'—You must agree to take those IUDs.'

Grobichov, relaxing, chuckled. 'Those fucking contraceptives again! Are they defective? Okay, no problem. We'll pay a fair price; our trade negotiators can work out the details . . . So—!' He stretched forward to offer O'Reilly his hand. 'We have a deal! *Chudno*! Of course, we're being too generous. You know that. England and France will still have their missiles. You strike a tough bargain, Mr President.'

The handshake came to an end at last. O'Reilly got unsteadily to his feet, trying not to grin. God, he had pulled it off! He wasn't sure why it was so important to off-load the contraceptives on to the Russians, but there had to be a good reason. 'Let's have some champagne!' he said.

'Excellent!'

In a hiss of ice the Dom Perignon emerged from the silver bucket. 'Better than a nuclear submarine breaking to the surface —eh, my friend?' purred Grobichov.

With trembling fingers O'Reilly tore at the wrappings. 'Here, let me,' offered Grobichov.

'You're damn right it is! It shows what can be done with good will. I know you're being generous. And I feel—I feel . . .' O'Reilly's eyes moistened unexpectedly. 'A kind of grace, Alex. You could say, that the spirit of Christ is with us in this room. Only, I guess, you don't believe in Christ.'

'As a good man—certainly.' Grobichov's face strained, turned red; the cork popped and hit the roof beams. Champagne creamed over the sides, chugged into O'Reilly's held-out glass.

Grobichov, too, was finding it difficult to disguise his joy. This was one in the eye for Kosygin! How astonishing that he, once a toiling coal miner in the Urals, should be at a summit, deciding the fate of the world! He scarcely listened to O'Reilly, chuntering about the closeness of God he always felt when standing by the Pacific. 'Golf in California' came through to him as 'Gulf of California'; 'play a round' with the Nixons came over as 'play around' with them . . . a foursome . . . But still the significance of the sexual revelation didn't break through to him until the President spoke questioningly the word 'games'. 'Oh, *da, da*!' he exclaimed, his jowls quivering in a delighted laugh. He had a picture of O'Reilly and Wanda lying on a huge round water-bed, naked with the Nixons. '*Konieshno*! Of course!'

Flames leapt in the hearth; champagne bubbled; the two men stood face to face in amity. 'To love, in all its forms, Vince!' chuckled Grobichov, raising his glass.

'Wonderful!' exclaimed O'Reilly. 'May it bring us still closer!'

He spoke of the marvels of California. The Russian said he had read about some of them. 'I read somewhere you own a huge limousine, the biggest in the world; with a bar and a jacuzzi, and red velvet love seats. Is it true, or just an invention by your media?' His eyes twinkled. 'Is that where you entertain the Nixons when you're at your beach house?'

'To love!' exclaimed the President, raising his glass, his eyes twinkling back.

'I'd like to have a limousine like that! And with a topless barmaid, I hear!'

'Well, sometimes,' O'Reilly admitted. 'If we feel like a drive after our game. It's a spectacular coastline.'

'You know, our sailors got to California before you, a couple of hundred years ago.' Grobichov chuckled merrily. 'You ought to give it back to us.'

'You shall have it. We'll give it to you.'

Chuckling still more merrily, the Russian gazed up at the President, expecting a grin; but he saw only intense seriousness. O'Reilly continued earnestly: 'You shall have it. You have my word. In the spirit of the Firebird.' He thrust out a big, horny hand.

'I was only joking,' gasped Grobichov, as his limp hand was crushed.

'I'd no idea your sailors got to California first. Well, in a couple of years, your young people can be walking through the streets of LA . . . And we'll have our limo crated up and shipped to Moscow before you can say Jack Robinson . . .' But Grobichov, overcome by orgasmic excitement and bewilderment, had already buckled at the knees; his glass slipped from his hand, and he crashed back into his armchair, gasping for breath.

'Are you okay?' enquired O'Reilly in alarm. 'It's warm here. Just stay where you are, I'll go call one of the guards . . .'

He stumbled to the door, threw it open, and barked an order. A security guard barked into his intercom. Within moments Mako and a doctor were running down the path. But Grobichov was already standing at the door, taking deep breaths of cold air, and saying he was okay, it had just been the stuffiness. The American doctor insisted on examining him, and they went inside. O'Reilly took the opportunity to tell Mako about the breakthrough. The IUD, and nuclear withdrawal from Europe inside two years. Mako expressed muted pleasure, though within he was dancing for joy. True, the old man had gone further with disarmament than they'd planned, but it was worth it to have the Soviets agree to the Independent Unilateral Defence initiative. God knows how he'd pulled it off—and to think that, only a few weeks ago, they'd been thinking they'd have to fix him up with a lead overcoat!

'You've done a terrific job, Tiger!'

'I've not done so badly for an old has-been—do you think?'

The icy wind from Lake Geneva stung their faces, yet they both felt warmed and exhilarated.

'Oh, and he's confirmed the Soviets will be at the '84 Olympics.'

'That's wonderful!'

The doctor emerged. 'Comrade Grobichov's fine, Mr President.'

Mako thanked him, then gladly acccpted O'Reilly's invitation to come in and have a celebratory glass. They found the Russian leader standing, sipping champagne, looking as healthy as a dog once more. 'You okay?' asked Mako solicitously. He was fine, said Grobichov; no problem. He poured Mako a drink. The three men toasted the successful negotiations.

'Did you tell him about California?' Grobichov asked O'Reilly, preparing to chuckle at the good joke.

'Yes, I've just heard it,' said Mako. 'And I'm very pleased. The world's had enough of recriminations and barriers. "Something there is that doesn't love a wall." Our poet Frost said that to Khrushchev at the time you were building the Berlin Wall. It's good to see the walls begin to come down, sir.'

His face paling, Grobichov sank down into his chair. The Americans sat too. Mako's brain was bubbling like the Dom Perignon. He happened to have large holdings in the TV company which owned the rights to the Olympics, and he was calculating that he was about three million dollars richer as a result of the Russians' decision to attend. He threw a log on the fire, and gazed dreamily at the flames. How good life was! The coldly copulating Makos who, so family legend said, had started his line, could never have dreamt he would be drinking champagne here, at the fireside summit . . .

Grobichov was earnestly and almost defensively telling the story of an early Russian landing at San Francisco. Nikolai Petrovich Rezanov had landed there in 1806—forty years before the Americans were strong enough to seize California from the Spaniards. 'If Rezanov hadn't had the bad luck to get himself killed in Siberia on his way home,' said Grobichov, 'it's certain he'd have persuaded the Emperor to let him establish a colony.'

'I know about it,' replied Mako. 'I even wrote an essay on

it once, when I was at Princeton. He got himself engaged to the Commandant's daughter—am I right? And when he didn't return, she became California's first nun.' He concluded jokingly: 'Its only nun!'

Grobichov shrugged. 'I didn't know about that.'

'So there's a strong political connection,' said Mako. 'It would be a shame if your flag weren't flying in LA.'

Grobichov hunched forward, staring down at his clasped hands. Spasms of cramp had seized his stomach. What the Americans were agreeing to was beyond belief, and yet undeniable. O'Reilly and Mako were both solemnly nodding. He felt nauseous with excitement and bewilderment. The agreement was too momentous to be discussed now; he'd have to talk about it with Bogdanovich and the others. They'd never believe it. Lifting his face he asked, 'How will the Californians respond?'

'Oh,' said Mako, 'there'll be a few right-wing nuts who will try to make things difficult; but generally you'll get a warm welcome. It'll have to be well-organized, but I can assure you it will be.'

'They're an unpredictable race,' said the President. 'Almost a separate country. But I don't envisage any real problems: do you, Walter?'

'No. I don't.'

Grobichov licked his dry lips. 'Well, we must talk further.' He rose unsteadily. 'And we continue to keep everything under wraps till we sign an agreement in the morning and give our press conference.'

'Naturally, sir.'

Grobichov and O'Reilly put on their coats; then the former proposed one final toast to peace and co-operation. After gulping, he hurled his glass at the wall, and the Americans followed suit. They left the historic lakeside house and strolled, one behind the other, up the path. The cameramen were waiting.

The leaders pumped hands again, and wore friendly smiles, though Mako's face was noticeably sombre.

'It's all cosmetic,' guessed the *Los Angeles Times* reporter. 'Look at Mako for the true account.'

'You're probably right,' grunted his San Francisco colleague.

'See you tonight,' said Grobichov as the pumping hands separated. He stooped to enter the armour-plated Zil. The motorcade moved off. Grobichov sank back, exhausted, exhilarated, perplexed.

Doubt had also gripped the mind of Mako. His doubts increased, like the dusk beginning to mask the mountains, as he jogged later with two fit security guards. The Soviets had 'bought' their arms deal at far too high a price. As Lyndon Johnson had once said, whoever controlled space controlled the world. Did Grobichov seriously believe that, having done all the research, the US would give up that power? Very unlikely! So—he thought, as his breaths rasped—maybe they knew something America didn't. Had started space research themselves, and found it wouldn't work?

Yet Mako had talked to over a dozen top scientists, in top installations from New York to Silicon Valley, and they'd all agreed that—though the idea had never occurred to them—it was absolutely, brilliantly feasible. Clearly, O'Reilly's 'antimatter rays' were in reality laser beams; the old man was always vague on detail. The scientists, sworn to secrecy, had become highly excited on the phone, hoping for a piece of the action. It would take a long time, a lot of dough, they all thought: a veritable Manhattan Project. But that had worked out; and so, they were confident, would this.

Then, what was Grobichov playing at? An attack in Europe when the missiles were gone and before IUD arrived? Mako's feet pounded, his heart pounded. That had to be it . . . Had O'Reilly given away too much? They'd have to tread very carefully . . .

He had dinner that evening at the Intercontinental Hotel with the First Lady's pleasant interpreter. And afterwards, up in her room, he screwed her. Far away from the fading wife and the boringly significant other, they enjoyed the adventure. Yet his thoughts kept straying to the IUD, and the dangers. Indeed, the only time he was completely hers was when he spunked into her—taking it for granted she was on the Pill.

· 17 ·

As dusk was falling over Calvin's thriving commercial city, Larissa Grobichov lay naked on her bed, rubbing between her thighs and writhing. The Soviet leader straddled a chair, resting his chins on his shirtsleeved arms. He was not watching her, but staring blankly at a wall.

'Make love to me, Alexei,' she pleaded.

'There isn't time, darling,' he murmured. 'And I have too much to think about.'

'You've lost interest in me,' she said sadly.

He gave an uncertain headshake. Larissa groaned, her body arched off the bed; she lay still, her hand fell away.

'What's their game?' he asked the blank wall. 'California! Offering us California! And giving us all we want on Europe . . . I know I'm being made a fool of, but I don't know why or how.'

'Have you rung Kosygin?'

'He just laughed when I told him about California. As you did! I know what he's thinking—I'm a novice, and serve me right for not having him along . . . But what am I missing,

Larissa? Help me . . . Use your fucking psychology . . .'

She wound herself in a duvet and supported her head on her elbow. 'Well, I think O'Reilly is almost childishly straight-forward. Of course his mind is in poor shape. There may even be some kind of neurological damage I can't put my finger on. But I don't see him as essentially deceitful, Alexei. You remember that American psychoanalytical paper I showed you? By someone called Greenbaum.'

'No, I don't.'

'It suggested O'Reilly had somehow become incapable of lying.'

'Oh, yes. It was crazy.'

'Well, I'm not sure. An old man, sick of a lifetime of lies and trickery, can have an illness characterised by total truth-telling. And at the same time, total generosity. King Lear . . .'

'You're not telling me O'Reilly is King Lear!' Grobichov sneered. 'And certainly Mako isn't. Throw me my cigarette case, would you? And my lighter . . . No, I have the feeling it's to do with Saltikov-Shchedrin. If he really did spy for them, they may have our whole defence system blown wide open. It's terrifying. It would explain why they're playing with us, kidding us along . . .' For the first time, he turned his piercing eyes on Larissa. 'You've *got* to find out the truth for me, Larissa.'

The young woman shivered, as from an attack of goose pimples. 'You use people,' she said. 'You use *me*.'

'And you love it.'

'Did you really destroy him for nothing?'

'Not for nothing. For Russia. He was ancient. We've had enough old men. But I may have been wiser than I knew. God help us, if so! How can we find out?'

He stood up from his straddling position, and waved his cigarette at her. 'We'll use the Fedorov strategy!'

'It'll never work.'

'Why not? You said it worked in the Serbsky.'

'Yes, but with men who were deranged, and who knew about Fedorov.'

'Well, we'll make sure he knows about Fedorov. We'll give Wanda a nice sleep. And you can derange him, my dove!'

He caressed her cheek with his finger, then lifted the bedside phone and dialled. As he waited and smoked, he scrutinised Larissa's face like a portrait painter. He spoke: 'Rykov, I want a good make-up artist here.' He replaced the phone.

'Your mother will have to eat in her room,' he said. 'She won't mind, will she?'

'Well, it's very rude,' said Larissa. 'She was looking forward to dining with the President of the United States. —Oh, but I don't suppose she'll mind. She'd feel awkward, and she hates rich foods. I'll tell her she can order what she likes, and choose whatever film she wants to see on video.'

'Is she having a good time, do you think?'

'Yes, except she's homesick.'

· 18 ·

The two couples dined intimately, untroubled by interpreters. Wanda having fully recovered, and the negotiations having produced an accord beyond anyone's dreams, all four were in a relaxed and happy mood. Conversation flowed as easily as the red Georgian wine. The O'Reillys talked of their career in the movies and found, in Larissa especially, an eager listener. She was enamoured of the cinema. She loved Bergman's films above all, she said: an opinion, enthusiastically endorsed, which brought a promise from the Tiger that he'd give her a copy of the latest *Digest*.

He crooned a few phrases from *Casablanca*, as Larissa, in a tight red dress, flashed askance at him her blue eyes, full of Russian yearning. Her lips were speaking of Bergman's sombre vision, but her eyes spoke something else—something that made his head spin. Ungainly movements of his arm, in picking up his wineglass, told him that her flesh, under the intoxicating red dress, was as firmly encased as the night before. He recalled Grobichov's unbelievable offer, 'Do you want my wife?'

Ah, it was just a dream! Such miracles didn't happen. Her

eyes were playing with him, teasing him. He was an old
man. She would laugh about him later with Grobichov. And
anyway, there was Wanda. Yet Wanda seemed unconcerned
—she was joking and flirting with the balding sparkly eyed
Russian leader, across the table. They were closer in age than
was any other pairing at the dinner table, O'Reilly reminded
himself. Grobichov seemed to enjoy her. Maybe he liked
overdressed ageing women plastered in rouge.

The air of jollity and flirtation was interrupted by a message
delivered to Grobichov. He spoke briefly, gravely, to his wife
in Russian—her face became sorrowful—then he explained to
his guests what had happened. A little boy at the children's
home, which Larissa had visited, had been drowned. A Soviet
journalist had taken the lad out, as a treat; by the river he had
run away, and slipped over the bank. The journalist had jumped
in after him, but the Rhône was swift-running. The journalist,
Spassky, had almost lost his own life. No one else had been
around, to lend a hand. Spassky was in a hospital, shocked and
distraught.

'How awful!' said Wanda; and Larissa, clearly shaken, said
she'd been present when Spassky had made his kind proposal
to the teacher. She had encouraged it. Larissa covered her face
with her hands.

'You mustn't blame yourself,' said her husband. 'It's tragic.
And it's an unfortunate incident. But obviously it wasn't anyone's fault, and our pressman did all he could.'

'I feel sorry for him,' Wanda said. 'He's going to have to live
with this for the rest of his life.'

'I must go and see him before we leave,' murmured Larissa.

'Yes, that would be a nice gesture, my dear. And I'll send a
note to the Swiss Prime Minister expressing our condolences.'

'At least,' sighed his wife, 'the little boy presumably had no
family to grieve over him. They were all abandoned children,
battered children.'

'How sad!' sighed Wanda. In some ways, she suggested, it made it seem worse. To be abused by your parents, and then die like that, so young.

Yes, what had been the point of his little life? asked Larissa. Sadly they sipped their wine, and toyed with their sturgeon. 'Death . . .' intoned the Russian leader. 'That's the real enemy, my friends. Not'—his sleek hand gestured from O'Reilly, facing him, to Larissa—'America or Russia.'

His wife nodded; said, in an exalted tone, 'I hate death, like Tsiolkovsky.'

'I love his music,' said Wanda. 'The *Swan Lake*.'

'Not Tchaikovsky. Tsiolkovsky. I was quoting our poet Yevtushenko. Tsiolkovsky was the first man to pioneer research into space travel, fifty or more years ago. He had a dream of filling the whole universe with life, human life. One day it will happen.'

Grobichov gave a grunt of assent, and prodded his fork in O'Reilly's direction. O'Reilly, day-dreaming, jerked back his head. 'Our countries should be co-operating in space, my friend!' Grobichov growled. 'We'd have been happy to do so, but you were bent hell to get to the moon first.'

'Hell bent,' his wife corrected. He shrugged.

'You could be right,' conceded O'Reilly. 'But I wasn't in power then, remember.'

'But you're in power now, my friend. And you and I—all of us—trust each other and are friends. Could we not . . .' He leaned back to let a servant take his plate. 'Could we not . . . cement our accord by working together on some great humanitarian project?' His eyes, solemn a moment before, sparkled joyfully.

'Tiger, that's a *wonderful* idea!' the First Lady exclaimed, stretching across to touch his hand. 'Don't you agree?'

'It would be wonderful!' Larissa enthused.

'I agree.'

Grobichov clicked his fingers in delight. 'I've got it! Fedorov! What do you think, Larissa?'

She frowned. She thought it was a stupid idea. He knew she'd never put any faith in it. The research was a waste of money.

'You're wrong. They've already done some exciting work. They think it could come true within thirty years. If we had American technology behind us, we could halve the time.'

He had thrown back his head; his delighted eyes were fixed on the ceiling.

'Who is this Fedorov? What research? Thirty years for what to come true?' The O'Reillys glanced, bewildered, from Grobichov to his wife.

Larissa smiled ironically. 'Alexei has big dreams. A lush imagination. Everything must be grandiose. Like all our rulers, from Peter the Great down . . .'

'Nikolai Fedorov,' explained her husband, delving into a dish of cranberries, 'was a nineteenth-century scientist.'

'Mystic!' Larissa corrected contemptuously.

Grobichov shrugged. 'Call him what you like. He was a great thinker. He influenced Tolstoy and Dostoievsky. A librarian for most of his life at the Rumyantsev in Moscow. His dream . . . was to resurrect the dead.'

'Resurrect the dead!' repeated Wanda incredulously.

'What, all of them?' O'Reilly exclaimed.

'Everyone who's ever lived.'

'You see why I said it was stupid,' said Larissa.

'He believed it was the solemn, sacred task of humanity to bury their differences and unite in that great labour, of bringing the dead to life.'

'Everyone who ever lived! Boy oh boy . . . !'

'How did he ever imagine it could be done, Alex?' asked Wanda.

'By harnessing the forces of nature, like electricity. Of course he didn't know about atomic energy.'

'It was completely crazy, Wanda,' Larissa said. 'It had no scientific foundation. It was all going to happen in extra-terrestrial space!'

'Well, so what?' her husband said, pointing his spoon heaven-ward. 'That's by no means crazy! The point is, there'd be so many people . . .'

'Yes, and at what point would one start, Alexei? With ape-men? At what point on the evolutionary ladder do you draw the line? Would you exclude aborted foetuses?'

'Don't be silly, Larissa.'

'I'm not being silly. They're human. And these contracep-tives which we've agreed to buy from the Americans, they actually produce abortions. They attack the fertilised egg—at least that's what they think. I checked in a library this morning.'

'Really?' said Wanda, looking anxious.

'Yes. If it's in the womb, this thing, it can hardly be stopping the sperm from reaching the egg.' She turned back to her husband. 'So are you going to resurrect all those embryos, killed off by an IUD?'

'I'm not saying there wouldn't be problems. But you've gone way ahead, darling. The main thing is—isn't it a wonder-ful vision of the future? In a hundred years or so, people are going to be immortal, medical science will have solved the problem of ageing . . .'

'Of course.' Larissa shrugged. 'That's inevitable.'

Wanda, dismayed, said she wasn't sure she liked that idea. It seemed to go against God's will, that we should meet up in heaven if we lived a good life. But Grobichov, in his excited vision, swept over her doubts, describing a world in which there would be no more death, and in which all would unite to bring life again to those who had not been so lucky. Everyone alive, as in Fedorov's vision; and peopling the stars and constellations, as in Tsiolkovsky's vision. And at the Fedorov Scientific Institute in Tambov they had already made progress. From an analysis of the DNA of one Soviet family, they had been able to calculate the DNA-structure of a long-dead grandfather. If the Soviet Union and United States combined their resources and talents on such a vast humanitarian project —would it not bury for ever their animosities, making their political differences seem petty? 'What do you say, Mr President?'

O'Reilly felt Larissa's hand brush his thigh. It didn't seem accidental. A shiver ran along his spine.

'What do you say? Wanda'—Grobichov turned to the worried First Lady—'you are bothered about heaven. But if there is a God, and if there is a heaven—perhaps God wants us to help Him in creating that heaven?'

'I guess you could be right. After all, he gave us our brains.'

'Precisely!'

'We'll do it!' exclaimed the President. He thrust his hand across the table. Grobichov shook it feverishly. 'Wonderful! We'll announce it tomorrow, if that's okay with you? Let's aim to resurrect the first . . . corpse by the year 2000!'

He raised his glass and proposed a toast to Nikolai Fedorov. 'To Fedorov,' repeated the Americans awkwardly.

'Larissa?'

'—*Khorosho*. To Fedorov.'

O'Reilly was calculating. By the year 2000 he would probably be dead himself. His feelings were therefore mixed when Grobichov suggested, wholly seriously, that the first person resurrected should be the little boy swept away by the Rhône that day.

· 19 ·

They sprawled on sofas in a quiet lounge. A chamber piece by Aaron Copland, grating but mercifully quiet, was playing. A servant tiptoed in with coffee and brandy decanter. Larissa poured the coffee; Alexci, the brandy, which he said came from Armenia.

Seated next to Wanda, his short legs resting on the coffee table, he took out a notebook and pen and started scribbling. 'I'm getting down our agreement,' he explained. 'Might I suggest we set out a programme of intent?' His alert eyes fixed on the sprawled-out, tired-looking President. '2000 for the first resurrection. 2050 for a full-scale resurrection in space? How does that strike you, Tiger?'

'This brandy's good.'

Larissa touched the President's thigh in an amused gesture. 'Vince is being tactful, Alexei. What he really means is, you're making Peter the Great seem like an unimaginative little clerk.'

Grobichov grinned; said you got nowhere if you didn't set impossible goals.

'I'd go along with it,' mumbled O'Reilly.

'Boy!' murmured Wanda. 'This stuff sure is strong! My head's going round.' She reached to put down her brandy balloon; the Russian took his feet off the coffee table. 'I think I'll just rest a little,' she said, leaning back against the cushions, her eyes closing.

'It's not so strong,' said Grobichov. 'Probably it's because you've not been well.'

'What time is it?' asked O'Reilly. 'Maybe we should go.'

Larissa pressed his knee; said it was still early. He relaxed. His wife, half opening her eyes, took off her shoes, curled her legs up, turning to face Alexei. 'I feel real sleepy,' she mumbled. Her eyes blinked into his, and shut. He stroked her arm. 'Then have a nap,' he said.

Within a few minutes, quiet snores were coming from her; her mouth was open. Her companions smiled at her. 'It's no wonder she's tired,' murmured Grobichov, 'after what happened last night.' He yawned. 'Actually, I feel quite tired too.' He put his feet up on the coffee table once more, and closed his eyes. His plump white-shirted stomach rose and fell gently, bulging over his waistband.

Within moments, he too was breathing deeply and nasally.

'Like the babes in the wood!' O'Reilly murmured, smiling. 'Well, it's been a hard two days.'

'It works extremely well. Would you like some more brandy?'

She picked up the decanter and refilled their glasses.

'Ah, isn't this peaceful!' she said, snuggling closer.

'What works extremely well?'

'I drugged their coffee.'

'I shouldn't drink any more.'

'I wanted us to be alone.'

'You *what*?'

She pressed her mouth to his. He touched her hard, stiff body under the sliding silk dress. He shivered.

'I want you,' she murmured. 'Is it bad of me? I've wanted you ever since we met.'

O'Reilly pulled away, and stammered, 'But this is wrong. And I'm old . . .'

'Age is all in the mind. You're powerful. And you could be cruel, I know. Cruel in the tenderest way. I told you, that excites me. And I feel I excite you too, don't I?' Her fingers stroked his groin; her mouth clung fast; he moaned.

'Come.'

'Yes,' he gasped, 'you know you do turn me on—you bitch.'

'Ah, yes!—yes! Abuse me!'

'You know, he offered you to me, this afternoon.'

'That doesn't surprise me. He isn't interested in sex. Come!' She took his hand and led him, stumbling, to a side door. It opened to a bedroom. She closed the door behind them, then fumbled at his tie. O'Reilly swayed; his eyes glazed; he made choking sounds. 'Let me undress you, my darling,' she crooned, 'like your mama used to.'

When she had stripped him naked, she crossed her arms, caught hold of her dress at the hips and peeled it off in a single movement. He stared at the rapturous vision, her torso trapped in the sleek tight black corselette, bought in Geneva, her bosom and hips outswelling above and below the clenched waist. His brawny hands could almost encircle that waist; he gripped her there, moaning softly, and covered her white, half-exposed globes with kisses. Then, crouching clumsily, he pressed his mouth to the blonde pubic hair, in its frame of tight garter-straps, soft bulging flesh. 'I love you, Larissa!' he groaned. 'I'm your slave!'

She stroked his mop of red hair—so striking a contrast to the grey sprouting from his chest. 'That's not what I want,' she murmured. 'You should know that, Tiger. Here—tie me to the bed.' She reached behind her to slide open a drawer. 'I have some straps. We seem to have everything in our

Mission . . .' She moved back—O'Reilly's hands caught him from falling forward—and threw herself on the bed. It was a small bed; it might originally have been a child's bed even; when she kicked off her high heels and spreadeagled her limbs, her hands and black-hosed feet touched the four bedposts. O'Reilly, in a mist, a delirium of passion, pulled himself to his feet. He found the straps, and with frantic, shaking hands fumbled them on her, binding her fast.

'Tighter! Tighter! I could pull myself free!'

'God, Larissa, look at me! It's been ten years since—'

He tightened the straps. She writhed, arching from the bed, struggling to escape. He knelt between her legs, stroking her hard nipples.

'Do you think I'm a whore?'

'No—yes! You're a whore!'

'I am, I am! You bastard American, you'll pull my tits off! I guess you think I deserve it. You want to humiliate me! You've got me right where you want me. You've got my cunt spread wide where you can see it, shove anything you like up in me!'—She twisted and bucked, pulling at her bonds. 'But I deserve it. I'm a filthy Russian tart. I deserve all I get.'

'I ought to piss in your mouth, you dirty whore!' growled O'Reilly.

Larissa moaned in joy. 'Oh yes! Piss on me! Shit on me!'

Lifting her head, her neck muscles straining, she spat. O'Reilly flicked at his eyes; slapped her left cheek hard, then her right; cried, 'I'll do more than piss and shit on you, you Communist turd! I'm going to wup you! To within an inch of your life—or maybe beyond.'

'Bastard, bastard!' she moaned, writhing. O'Reilly, looking around in vain for a whip, made do with pulling on her garter-straps, like tensing a bow, and then letting them zing against her thighs. She hissed with pain; cried, 'Is that the best you can do, you motherfucking Yankee prick? You're not a real master. My first lover and his pals used to shove a broken bottle up me. I had to go to hospital twice. They were real men, they were . . . real Russian men, not Yankees sissies like you!'

O'Reilly growled and, as he pulled viciously at her nipples, plunged his penis into her. He lunged and lunged, his old heart pounding in his chest. 'That'll come later,' he panted. 'Worse than that! After I've used you to jerk off in! I love you . . .'

'No, you just want to use me.' She spat again, straight into his eyes. He lunged still harder; bit her nipple . . . But something was different; she was no longer thrashing her head in anguished pain, but gazing in terror past his shoulder. O'Reilly paused, looked round. Grobichov stood in the doorway, swaying drunkenly, his face swollen with rage, his eyes bulging out of their sockets.

'*Bozhe moi*!' Larissa whimpered. O'Reilly, feeling his throat making a croaking noise, disengaged from her. He tried to stand up. Grobichov walked unsteadily towards him. 'Alex, I'm sorry, I—' O'Reilly began, but the Russian cut him short. 'You bastard! So this is trust! You could have asked; then you could have slept with her with pleasure, if my wife was willing. But not in this way!'

He was taking out his cigarette case; removing a cigarette from one end, putting it between his lips. 'No, Alexei, please don't!' Larissa whimpered. Her husband was crouching in front of O'Reilly, tilting the cigarette up, aiming at his throat.

'Alex, please!' O'Reilly begged the bloated, purplish face. But the lips puffed out; and the Tiger crumpled to the floor.

Stepping round him, Grobichov calmly unstrapped his wife's hands and feet. She swung off the bed and began chafing her wrists and ankles. He crouched over the President, checking him rapidly.

'He'll sleep like a baby for twenty minutes.'

'Disgusting old man! Why didn't you come sooner?'

'I was enjoying it too much!' He pulled down a stiff cup of her corselette, which she had just pulled up, and twitched her hard nipple. 'I'd say you enjoycd it too!'

She tossed her head angrily. 'Go and get changed,' he said. 'Sosnitskaya's waiting for you; it won't take her long.'

She plucked a bathrobe from a hook and put it on. As she was checking her face before a mirror—wiping away a crystalline tear, smoothing her hair, dabbing her lips—Grobichov lifted a phone and grunted an order. Larissa glided through the room where Wanda slept placidly on the sofa. Two expressionless Cossack servants entered the bedroom through another door. Grobichov, smoking, indicated with a finger the crumpled body. Their lack of expression didn't alter as they picked up the large naked President and carried him out.

· 20 ·

Resurrected, as in Fedorov's vision,
Our ancestors will come to us.
YEVTUSHENKO

O'Reilly came round in a plain white-walled room without
windows. He was lying in a bed; he was wearing a kind of
nightshirt, and was covered by a sheet. Sleepy, muzzy-headed,
at first he thought the room was empty, but then he noticed
there was a woman sitting to his left. He could see only her
sandals, bare legs, and the hem of her skirt; the rest of her was
hidden by the newspaper she was reading. He saw, through
his long-sighted eyes, a title in Russian letters. He knew they
spelt *Pravda*.

The terrible scene he had just lived through came back to
him, slowly, and as if from another world. With that memory,
he groaned. The woman dropped her newspaper. She smiled
and murmured tenderly, 'Ah, you're awake, my dear, at
last!'

It was as if he couldn't focus on her. He blinked several
times; but her face was still troubling. This was, and was not,
Larissa Grobichov. Her features were clearly Larissa's; yet her
hair was almost entirely grey; her forehead was lined; her firm

and graceful chin had sagged; her blue eyes, gazing out through puffy flesh, lacked all lustre. Her body, in a somewhat shapeless brown frock, had thickened; that proud uptilted bosom had sagged.

He groaned again. 'Where am I?'

She smiled, and pulled her chair close to the bed. 'You're in Tambov,' she said softly.

'What's happened?'

'Ssh! All in good time. Don't become agitated.'

'Where the hell is Tambov?'

'In Russia. Tell me, my dear, do you remember anything from your past?'

'What's happened to you?'

'Ah, you remember me! That's wonderful!' She clasped her hands.

'Of course I remember. Why shouldn't I?'

A railway engine hooted somewhere in the distance. 'Tambov is a big railway junction,' she explained. 'Tell me—this is very important—do you remember what happened to you in Geneva?'

'I remember you—what a strange question! But you're different; you look older.'

'I know. Forget that, for a moment. Listen.' She stroked his hand. 'Listen to me quietly, without agitating yourself. You remember we were making love, and my husband burst in, and—'

'Could I forget it!' he groaned. 'Look, where the fuck am I? In a hospital?' His eyes, wandering, had noticed what seemed to be some kind of scanner, flashing a zigzag line, above the bed.

'Not exactly a hospital, but sort of. Don't worry, you're going to be all right.'

'My God, he shot at me with that cigarette of his!'

She nodded sadly. 'Yes. He didn't understand. He thought

you'd forced me to do it. Afterwards, he was almost mad with grief.'

'Then he didn't kill me?' His staring eyes roamed the room.

Larissa ignored his question, 'This is a wonderful moment,' she said, squeezing his hand. 'You've been in and out of consciousness for weeks, Tiger. But you had no idea who you were; your memory, your self-knowledge, hadn't come back. They thought if I came down from Moscow, seeing me might make the difference. And it has! I can't tell you how overjoyed I am! This is a great moment in history!'

'It must have looked awful!' He groaned again, and covered his face with his hands. 'I guess it's done for the summit.'

'No, that's where you're wrong. It actually made both sides more determined to make it a triumphant new beginning, in your mem—for your sake.' He dropped his hands, and she grasped them tightly between hers. 'And above all, they committed themselves to the great project. You remember—Fedorov's vision?'

'For weeks! Jesus Christ! Where's Wanda?'

'Don't get yourself worked up. She'll join you later. Not for weeks. For years . . .'

'Fedorov . . . Oh, resurrecting the dead.'

She nodded, gazed into his bleary, dazed eyes compassionately, tenderly, incredulously, joyfully. 'We worked on that—your country and mine. Threw all our resources into it. The arms race was over, you see.'

'Years!'

'Yes. Twenty years, to be exact. You're the second person to be—resurrected. The first was a little Swiss boy who was drowned—do you remember? That's what you agreed. I must admit, I was very sceptical about the project. Well, I was wrong. Thanks be to God, as mama used to say. You're at the Fedorov Institute. My husband was determined to work on you; but he didn't tell your wife or any Americans, because it might have seemed morbid and distasteful. We brought back just a sliver of your skin. But it was enough. Now do you begin to understand? I know this is difficult for you . . .'

She bent and kissed his wrinkled brow. O'Reilly's eyes darted about, fearful, perplexed. She continued, in the same anxious, tender tone: 'We hoped you'd be younger. But it seems you come back at the same age. However, you're better off than I.' She smiled mournfully. 'My beauty is gone. It's gone . . .'

'Jesus! You're pulling my leg!'

'No. No. Your remains are in Arlington Cemetery . . . Oh, I should reassure you, there was no scandal. Our people made it look like a heart attack, before sending for medical assistance. Your memory is greatly honoured.'

He struggled to sit up, but fell back. He felt as weak as a baby. 'Why aren't there any windows?' he demanded.

'Because you weren't supposed to have any sensory changes, in the early stages. Don't worry, now you'll soon be able to look out and go outside. And then, when you're strong, we'll announce the blessed news, and you can fly home to your country in triumph.'

O'Reilly tossed about, distraught, terrified. He couldn't believe it—yet there was the evidence of her face; and with an amused smile at his stubborn disbelief she showed him the copy of *Pravda*. He could read the date: October (it appeared) 23, 2002. And the Grobichov nightmare did seem an age away from this quiet room, this gentle grey-haired woman in a respectable, shapeless frock . . .

Gradually he began to accept it. And when he had adjusted to that reality, she broke the news of his wife's death. She had passed away peacefully ten years ago. But her death would be short-lived; she would join him in the not too distant future.

'Who's President now?'

She hesitated. 'Edward Kennedy.'

'And is Alex still in charge over here?'

'*Da.*'

'So Teddy made it at last!'

She showed him a hazy newspaper picture of his daughter. She wore glasses now, he saw, and her hair too was grey.

'Jesus Christ . . . Jesus Christ . . .' he mumbled, over and over. Then: 'Some people said we'd never see it through to the year 2000. Well, they were wrong!'

Larissa brought up, tentatively, a matter which had given her much pain over the years, and cast a cloud over her relationship with Alexei. The matter of the execution of Brezhenko's deputy, Saltikov-Shchedrin. She had always believed her husband had brought about his death for no offence, purely from ruthless ambition. But Alexei claimed he'd spied for America. She couldn't believe it was true. The old man had always seemed so upright and patriotic. It was all so long ago; if he *had* been a spy, there could no longer be any point in obscuring it. Any information he'd given to the Americans was totally out of date. She, Larissa, needed to know, one way or another, for the sake of her peace of mind.

He laid his hand on hers. Well, it couldn't make any difference now. Yes, he'd spied for the United States, for many years. He believed the CIA had 'turned' him in the late sixties, by laying some kind of sexual trap.

'Thank you. Thank you, my dear!' she murmured, kissing his brow. 'So then what my husband did is at least understandable, even if it was pretty ruthless. That makes me feel a lot better. And now you must get some rest. Your body is still in a very delicate condition. Someone should be coming to give you a small injection. Your drugs.'

His eyes rolled anxiously again. 'Who's the real me?' he demanded. 'Me, here, or that body in Arlington?'

'You. Here! There's no question!'

A white-uniformed male attendant slipped into the room. He looked at Larissa questioningly.

'Yes, he remembers!'

'*Chudno*! That's wonderful, Mr President! This won't hurt now. In a few minutes you'll drift off to sleep.'

He filled a hypodermic, pulled up O'Reilly's sleeve, and injected him. '*Spokoinoi nochi*! Good night!'

The orderly slipped out.

Larissa held O'Reilly's hand, and talked gently about their plans to welcome him in Moscow before his flight home. His eyes closed; he mumbled; he drifted off.

· 21 ·

I have had a most rare vision.
A MIDSUMMER NIGHT'S DREAM

Strident violins broke into O'Reilly's sleep. He stirred; slit open his eyes; he saw the comfortable lounge in the Soviet Mission; Wanda curled up, and Grobichov stretched out, asleep on the sofa; coffee pot and cups, and decanter of brandy. Turning his head, he saw Larissa, young and glamorous in her red dress. Her head was leaning back and her eyes were closed, but she was clearly not asleep: she balanced a coffee cup on her lap. O'Reilly touched his trousers, his shirt collar . . . All in order. Only his brain felt disordered, in a nightmare of confusion. Tambov . . . Fedorov . . . And before that, still scaringly vivid, Larissa bound and writhing . . . Grobichov's entry, his rage, his Sobranie . . .

Larissa opened her eyes and looked aside at him. She smiled. 'Ah, you're awake! Would you like some more coffee?'

O'Reilly mumbled and pulled himself up on the sofa. His head swam. There was a foul, stale taste in his mouth, as when one wakes in a plane after a short, unsatisfactory nap. 'It's probably cold,' she said; 'but I can send for some more.'

'Please.'

She stretched to pick up a phone, and rapped an order. Then

she sat back, moving closer to him, and stroked his trousered thigh. 'It's not a great compliment to me,' she said, 'falling asleep! Or is it just this record that's knocked everyone out? *I* think it's rather nice. I haven't heard it before.'

It was the same grating, contemporary chamber piece that had been scratching away before . . . 'How long was I asleep?'

'Quite a long time—fifteen minutes? I don't know. It's not surprising; even *I* feel drowsy . . . pleasantly so . . . and I haven't had to engage in high-powered negotiations . . . It's unusual for Alexei to nod off. The strain is telling.'

An expressionless servant with slanting Oriental eyes padded in bearing a coffee tray. Larissa thanked him and he withdrew. She poured O'Reilly's coffee and added cream. 'Another brandy?'

He waved away the offered decanter. 'That stuff is the devil's drink,' he mumbled. 'It gave me a wild dream.'

'Oh? Tell me about it. I'm interested in dreams.'

Grobichov was stirring. He yawned, rubbed his eyes, stretched up his arms; his eyes opening, his legs gave a jerk. '*Bozhe moi!* I was almost asleep,' he mumbled.

'Almost!' laughed Larissa. 'You've been snoring away for ages!'

'No. Impossible.' He pulled back his feet and sat up straight. 'I'm sorry, Mr President—you must think me very rude.'

'I dozed off too.'

Grobichov asked if there was any coffee left, and his wife said she'd had a fresh pot sent in. She re-filled his cup. Gulping the hot coffee, he surveyed the gently snoring Wanda with amused affection. The hardliners on both sides, he suggested, would be devastated if they could see how relaxed an atmosphere had grown up among the four of them; how informal and calm it was here. And no terrorists! he pointed out sardonically. Larissa added that she wished there'd been photos taken of the three of them snoozing away. Grobichov let out a bellowing laugh; it disturbed Wanda, who jerked awake in the middle of a snore. 'Goodness!' she mumbled, noticing how comfortably she was curled up. 'Have I been asleep long? I'm so sorry—you must think I'm treating your place as a hotel.' She slid her legs off the sofa, stood up, and brushed down her pink evening dress. Wobbling, still shaky, she collapsed back. Grobichov patted her hand. 'You needed it, my dear,' he said. 'Actually we've all had a nap—all except Larissa. Do you feel better?'

She nodded. 'Much fresher. But it just seems so rude of me.'

'Not at all. Have some more coffee.' He directed his gaze at the still drowsy President. 'Vince,' he said, 'I suggest we spend just a few minutes together, running through our agreements, ready for the morning. Do you agree?'

Larissa lamented that it would break up the peaceful atmosphere, but her husband assured her it would only take a few minutes. He rose, and offered his hand to help the old man out of the deep upholstery. He opened the inner door so fateful in O'Reilly's dream, and ushered him through. O'Reilly found himself in a neat, economically furnished study. There was a desk and three chairs; a low table on which rested writing paper and two pens. Lenin and Grobichov stared down sternly from framed portraits.

No sign of a bed, of course. Yet O'Reilly saw Larissa splayed out in her black corselette and hose—and felt the sweet plunge into her—as clearly as if it had happened. A sure sign of old age, he thought, when dreams outmatched reality.

Grobichov tugged a cord, pulling the drapes across, shutting out the night. Even the drapes and carpet were a different colour: drabber, more pragmatic. O'Reilly rubbed his groin. Soft, useless. An old man's fantasy of erection, resurrection.

Grobichov sat and invited him to sit opposite. He was suddenly all briskness and concentration; while the American, yawning, yearned only for his bed at the Maison Vichy. He declined the offered notepaper and pen. He'd forgotten to bring his reading glasses; he could hold everything in his head.

'So, my old friend,' began Grobichov, 'what have we agreed to?'

'You make the notes, Alec.'

'What are the main points of agreement?'

'The research project. Resurrecting the dead and colonising space.'

Grobichov assented to, yet downgraded, that matter with a single gesture. 'Naturally,' he said, 'we can only put it forward tentatively. We're both in the hands of our treasuries and our scientific establishments. Clearly there'll have to be a high-powered conference, sometime or other. Meanwhile, it would look pretty stupid if we announced we're going to try to resurrect the dead!' He flashed his brilliant, gold-filled teeth. 'I suggest a vague statement about collaborating in some kind of humanitarian space project. Okay?' He scribbled.

'And now we come to nuclear disarmament,' he continued. 'Europe a non-nuclear zone. Half our weapons to go now, half in two years' time.' He gabbled for several minutes about precise details of timing and verification, etc. O'Reilly nodded and yawned. He'd leave all that to Mako and Requiem. They were the experts.

Grobichov scribbled. Then, with a sly, questing smile he said, 'Do you want us to mention California?'

'Okay, Alec.'

The sly smile turned to sharp, probing stare. The guy was straight-faced—almost bored-looking. He was giving up California with an air of *ennui*.

'We'll make special arrangements, of course,' said the Russian leader.

O'Reilly nodded. 'Yes. That will reassure the organisers.'

Grobichov took out his cigarette case and lit up. O'Reilly jumped. Grobichov brooded. He hadn't even dared mention California to the rest of his team. They'd think he'd gone mad. 'I've been thinking,' he said at length, 'there are perhaps adjustments we can make along our borders. With the agreement of our East German allies, of course. When the East–West border was established, certain villages west of Magdeburg felt bad about being split off from their market centre, which was in the West. Of course, they've adjusted, and they'd probably object to losing their socialist way of life. But I think we might be generous; we might adjust the border around there to include them in West Germany. What do you say? I wish to be generous.'

'We'd expect you to make special arrangements for your own security—of course,' said the Tiger.

The Russian nodded. 'And for the villagers. There will be minefields to be cleared, and so on. But it can be done. Shall we put all this down as correcting certain anomalies in our borders? We don't need to be too specific. We don't want to frighten people.'

O'Reilly's weariness lifted. This was wonderful, unbelievable. He'd become famous as the President who started to undo the mistakes of Potsdam. 'Thank you,' he said cautiously. 'That's—that would be welcomed.'

The pen raced across the page. Grobichov paused to dab his high forehead with a handkerchief. He felt exhilarated yet uneasy. All hell would break loose in LA, San Francisco, Silicon Valley. Silicon Valley! Undreamed-of wealth and power. A socialist paradise! His fantasies raced. The Rezanov SSR, after the first Russian explorer to land on that seaboard. Hollywood renamed Eisenstein. A *dacha* at Malibu . . .

Yet—what the hell were they playing at? At this summit, the Americans were giving away more than any country in the history of the world, and were getting simply nothing in exchange.

He tapped his pen on the blotter, deeply perplexed. Mako had said yes too, and he was nobody's fool. O'Reilly's voice came from far away. 'Don't forget the IUDs.'

'Ah, yes. Shall we say a substantial quantity of contraceptives of the intra-uterine variety? At a price to be decided?' He scribbled 'IUD', and sat back, still more deeply perplexed. He would test the contraceptives on female prisoners.

'Is that it?' said O'Reilly.

'That's it!' Grobichov leaned across and they shook hands warmly.

'It shows what can be achieved when our fucking hardliners aren't around, Alec.'

'You're right!' Grobichov felt his anxieties ease, the blood course through his veins. At fifty-five, he could have thirty years of power ahead of him. Nothing was impossible. He *would* make Peter the Great seem like a clerk without imagination. He urged O'Reilly that they should tie up these negotiations that very night. Call up the Maison Vichy and get his team over; he would round up the Soviets. He believed in striking while the iron was hot. It was only eleven-thirty. The President, dazed, weary, was persuaded to lift the phone and have himself put through to his residence. He spoke to a junior aide, who told him a tarantula had been found and was flying from Paris. 'Get Mako, Requiem and Bloomfield over here right away. Find them!'

When they returned to the lounge, they found to their surprise that Olga Ivanovna, Larissa's mother, had joined the First Ladies. She was wearing dressing-gown and slippers, and her hair was wrapped in a towel. Rising to her feet to grasp O'Reilly's hand, she explained, through her daughter, that it would have been very rude of her not to come down and see them. They might think she wasn't grateful for being received as a guest in their house. She hoped they'd had a nice evening. There was a small, dried bloodstain on the President's neck, near his Adam's apple, and she insisted on licking her handkerchief and dabbing off the spot. Wanda said her husband always shaved carelessly.

· 22 ·

The rotund miner's wife had shuffled off to bed; the lounge had filled up with black-suited Russians, annoyed at having had their sleep disturbed; with black-suited Americans, even more sour at having to drag themselves considerable distances. In Mako's case, he had still been in bed in the Hotel Intercontinental when the command came. His interpreter friend had answered the phone, which was embarrassing. Requiem, a Baptist, and ambitious, was quite capable of leaking it to Mako's wife.

Interpreters ghosted around; but as yet the American voices and the Russian voices kept themselves separate. Waiters distributed coffee, tea, and various drinks. The tranquillity of the evening was shattered.

Larissa, fondling O'Reilly's lapel, lamented her husband's ceaseless energy. She'd have preferred a different end to the evening. 'Maybe it's stupid, but I hoped we'd have a chance to be alone together like last night, Tiger. You know I like you.' Her eyes gazed serenely up at him. He became flustered; choked on his reply. She sighed; said she guessed personal feelings had to give way to great issues. She was happy the summit had gone so wonderfully well.

Grobichov's broad back brushed against O'Reilly's, as he sipped orange juice and caressed Wanda with his mellifluous voice. Wearing a strained, fluttery smile, she was saying she'd love to show him Camp David. They would love to come, he said. She and the President must come to Moscow; and visit their lovely *dacha* in the Crimea. 'Oh, we'd love to!' And Wanda, reaching past him, tugged at Tiger's jacket hem. He swung round. 'Tiger, they've agreed to come and visit us!'

'And you're coming to Moscow!' Grobichov smiled.

'Oh, that's great! When?'

Grobichov shrugged. 'June?'

'We'd love to! Thank you!'

'Honey, I'd like a word with you. Excuse me.' She took her husband's hand and led him away. She looked anxious. 'I wanted to say to you, I'm worried about the IUDs you're going to sell the Russians.'

'What's wrong, sweetheart?'

'Something Larissa said at dinner. About them bringing on an abortion. I'm sure Katie doesn't know that. I'm going to talk to her when we get back, before she goes to the clinic.'

'Why are you worried?'

'You can imagine what the Friends of Life would say if they found out Katie was wearing an IUD. And what they'll say, honey, if you start selling them to the Soviets. Don't do it. Sell them something else.'

'Did Larissa say that?'

He felt his arm gripped. It was Grobichov. 'Tiger, I'm going to take my team into the study. You can talk to yours here. Then we'll get together round the table. Okay?'

He moved away, and started shepherding his aides towards the door. A servant tapped Wanda on the shoulder. Her limo was ready. She kissed Tiger on the cheek, wishing him luck, and thanked Larissa for a wonderful evening. Larissa clasped O'Reilly's hand, saying she was going to bed. She would see him in the morning. Her eyelashes fluttered some mysterious signal. He scratched an itching upper arm, and wistfully watched her glide from the room. His team gathered round him. He tried to collect his thoughts.

'Look, you guys,' he began, 'I know you set a lot of store by the IUD; but Wanda thinks it's kind of immoral. Couldn't we drop it?'

Mako snapped: 'Since when have US government policies been dictated by the First Lady?' Simultaneously Requiem exclaimed: 'She's talking a load of crap.'

O'Reilly, after a few moments' thought, said, 'Dammit, you're right, Walter! I'll tell her to go fuck herself.'

'But we're going to get a lot of people thinking that,' Mako warned. 'It might be advisable not to be too specific in our announcement. Simply refer to the deployment of technology in the interest of peace—or some such thing.'

'I'd go along with that,' said Requiem. 'Play it cool.'

'That sounds good,' said Tiger.

All three advisers expressed their growing uneasiness about a nuclear-free Europe. They'd go along with it, for the sake of the Soviets' agreement to the IUD, but with profound misgivings.

O'Reilly sprang his piece of good news on them: Grobichov's willingness to cede some villages on the East German border near Magdeburg. His aides were overjoyed and astounded. What had they asked for in exchange? Absolutely nothing, said O'Reilly. Grobichov had had a good dinner and was in a benign mood.

Mako proposed a toast, in vodka, to the old man. He sincerely meant it. After all the scandals and traumas of the previous weeks, the President had proved himself to be a master of negotiation. If only the allies had had him at Potsdam.

When O'Reilly mentioned the resurrection of the dead, they almost laughed themselves sick. It was an excellent joke, in the best traditions of dead-pan American humour.

From time to time they heard Russian voices raised in altercation next door, but their interpreters could not catch what was being said.

Grobichov's announcement of his trade-off—a few miserable East German villages for California—had been greeted, not only with incredulity, which was expected, but downright hostility. Kirillov, Kropotkin and Bogdanovich all piled in on him. If they let a few East German villages go, how would they quell the longing for so-called western freedom all along the border? Not only there, but throughout the satellite states? Not only in the satellite states, but in the annexed republics—Lithuania, Latvia, Estonia, etc? There would be no end to it.

And California—even if it came off, which was unimaginable—would be a poisoned gift. You couldn't have a single Republic a thousand times richer than any of the others. When the Soviets took over, there wouldn't be a single Californian left; they'd have fled east. Silicon Valley would be dismantled and removed. The Soviets would find a desert of abandoned cities. The transfer of power could wreck the Soviet economy. If Soviet populations were shipped in—think how poverty-stricken they'd look, compared with the neighbouring Yanks. And, despite the Rockies, that long border would be indefensible.

Grobichov was shaken. He'd sensed something was wrong, but hadn't thought it out. It was the second savage blow of the night—the first being the discovery that Saltikov-Shchedrin had indeed been a spy. Yet he was able to persuade his comrades to give him a chance to explore the amazing offer further, and to let the trade-off pass, under the vague prescription of 'certain border anomalies'. Nothing would be spelt out, nothing would be irrevocable.

And the great prize was a nuclear-free Europe. They forgave Grobichov his naivety for having achieved this momentous breakthrough.

When they'd settled their differences, Grobichov warned them of one issue which might come up. For reasons he couldn't divulge just yet, he had spun O'Reilly a yarn about the two countries collaborating on some scientific research . . . into the resurrection of the dead and the colonisation of space! Crazy old Fedorov! He expected chuckles from his grimly humourless team, and was not disappointed. If they should hear something about humanitarian research in space, he said, they should just let it pass, it was meaningless.

· 23 ·

The negotiators sat at a conference table. The meeting had not yet begun: they were waiting for Grobichov, who was making a couple of phone calls to Moscow. Out of the droning interchange, in English and Russian, either side the table, Kropotkin's voice emerged with sudden clarity, addressing his opposite number, Requiem—

'Ob'yasnitye, pojal'sta, shto takoye IUD. Kak ono deystvuyet Pochemu vy tak 'stremites' ego prodat'?'

'Can you please explain this IUD? How does it work? Why are you so anxious that we should buy it from you?' explained the American interpreter.

Henry Requiem grabbed a sheet of paper and a pencil, and tried to draw a circle. Lacking (whatever his other virtues) the precision of Giotto, who could draw a perfect circle with one free movement of his hand, Requiem produced what looked like a single-celled animal. While Mako was replying, 'Because it's in the interest of peace,' Requiem was saying, 'Imagine this is the earth.' Russian has the same word for *peace* and *earth*—*mir*—and the poor Russian interpreter, attempting to translate both sentences at the same time, left the final word of Requiem's remark unspecified. '*Yaitso?*' asked Kropotkin, frowning, gazing at the weirdly drawn circle: 'Egg?' translated the American interpreter, in a jocular tone; and Mako grinned. Requiem drew, with a flourish, a wider circle outside the egg, and explained, 'The IUD sets up a protective barrier around it. As soon as a missile is launched—it's annihilated.'

Missile—*metatel'noye orudie* or 'launched weapon'—was such a droll description of sperm that the Russians smiled, the first time they had been seen to crack their lips at the summit. They, too, saw that Requiem had a human face, and the exchange served to relax the stiff atmosphere.

'*Spasibo, Gospodin Rekviem.*'

'You're welcome.'

O'Reilly, watching with interest from his central seat, thought: 'So the egg isn't fertilized. Wanda was wrong. She thinks she knows everything.'

Grobichov strode in, and took his seat, murmuring an apology.

He proposed that the American team, as guests, set out a suggested formula for summarising their points of agreement, and then the Soviets would comment and, if necessary, they could thrash out a compromise. Since O'Reilly did not at once respond, and was nodding in evident exhaustion, Mako stepped smartly in: 'Shall I do the honours, Mr President? I've taken some notes.'

O'Reilly's head jerked up. 'That's a good idea. Thank you.'

The agreements Mako drily listed were as follows:

1. Our governments will co-operate in space research designed eventually to create a new technology of a humanitarian nature, for the benefit of mankind as a whole.

2. As soon as possible, each government will withdraw one half its nuclear weapons from Europe. Within two years of the completion of this stage, withdrawal of the remaining missiles

will commence, subject to the agreement having been fully adhered to by both sides.

3. Since it is mutually accepted that anomalies have arisen as a result of the Potsdam Summit, it is agreed that a joint working party will be set up to correct these anomalies by a re-defining of certain frontiers.

4. Our governments agree to expand the commercial and cultural links between our countries.

Even as he was speaking, Mako, an expert poker player, was sizing up the deadpan faces of the opposition. They remained surprisingly unperturbed by the space defence initiative, the IUD; Kirillov and Kropotkin even nodded slightly. There were no nods during his reading of point two, and it was clear to him they were already taking to pieces his re-writing of the disarmament agreement. Over the next point, he sensed a degree of unease, but no outright hostility. Giving up East German villages!—what game were they playing . . . ? Point four, of course, was uncontroversial.

Grobichov, his hands folded on the table, his protruding eyes focused intently, was likewise summing up the deadpan Americans. Save for O'Reilly, they obviously knew the 'Fedorov' space collaboration was a farce, but they were ready to go along with it as a token of harmony and progress. They didn't expect to get away with their clumsy re-vamp of the key arms agreement. They remained serenely indifferent to the loss of California—yet watchful; perhaps wondering if the Reds had spotted the trap. And, for some reason, they didn't want to specify the sale of their contraceptives.

Clearing his throat, he broke the silence which followed Mako's summary: 'On point four, concerning commerce, you don't wish to be more specific?'

Mako said he didn't think so. Grobichov nodded assent. If they were back-pedaling on the accursed IUDs, or wished to hide the sale from their own people, so be it.

The Soviets agreed without debate to points one, three and four. But, as expected, a sour battle was joined over the all-important second point. O'Reilly, struggling to stay awake, took no part in it; and Grobichov stayed cool, rarely intervening. But around them, American voices rasped, and Soviet fists pounded. When the argument had been raging for half an hour, O'Reilly stirred himself to exclaim, 'That's enough! You guys piss me off! Both sides! The world is waiting for a message of hope from us, and all you can do is try to wreck everything Mr Grobichov and I have done.'

'Well said, Mr President!' said the Soviet leader. 'I agree absolutely. I've brought a load of shits and layabouts to Geneva with me, and so have you. I suggest you pricks take yourselves off somewhere, and resolve your differences. We want you back here in twenty minutes with a deal worked out. Otherwise I don't care if you have to stay up the whole fucking night— you're going to resolve it.'

Chastened, the six aides stole away, with their interpreters. Grobichov and O'Reilly sat face to face. They felt a deep intimacy envelop them. They were on the same side, against all the rest, all the warmongers. Their hands touched across the table. O'Reilly withdrew his quickly, embarrassed by an almost sexual tingling. He wanted to fling his arms around this man in a passionate, loving embrace; he could imagine wrestling with him naked by the fire in that little cabin.

Mumbling in embarrassment and weariness—it was two a.m.—he commented that the IUDs hadn't been mentioned. They were covered by the last point, Grobichov replied. Presumably Mako didn't want them mentioned specifically for some reason.

'Also, we've not mentioned your coming to the Olympics.'

Grobichov grinned. 'We hardly need to specify *that*! Wild Caucasian horses wouldn't keep us away!'

'Oh, of course!' exclaimed O'Reilly. 'Mako's a Catholic.'

'What? Oh, I see—contraceptives. There's a hell of a lot of hypocrisy in politics, Tiger. Ah, they're back already! You see, they only wanted their heads knocked together.'

'That's great.' O'Reilly swung round in time to see the chastened negotiators filing in.

'Are you awake? We signed an agreement, my dear.'

'*Chudno!*' Olga Ivanovna whispered sleepily, moving her rotund body so he could crawl into bed beside her. Grobichov sighed happily in her engulfing warmth as she cuddled him against her flannel-nightied bosom.

He fell asleep at once. The plain, homely woman continued to rub his back tenderly, as she had done almost every night for the past thirty-four years. She whispered, 'You may need her for show, but it's me you come to bed with at night . . .' She knew a lot of people would be shocked if they knew his 'grandson', little Stiva, was the child of a former mistress. They'd be much more shocked if they knew what he did with his daughter. Yet that wasn't so uncommon in tight-knit mining communities.

Oh, it had bothered Olga Ivanovna at first, when they returned from the Union trip to Poland and she knew something had happened between them. But one can grow resigned to anything in time. Alexei had never thrown her aside—simple-minded and dull as she was . . .

And besides, great Russian leaders, from Ivan the Terrible to Stalin, hadn't lived the lives of shopkeepers, and you couldn't expect them to. Big men had big appetites.

She was grateful to have come on this trip. And to have met the President of the United States!

Olga Ivanovna went on rubbing her husband's back; until she drifted off to sleep again . . .

Elsewhere, Larissa Alexeyevna dreamed; and never more richly. From Gorky to Geneva, her dreams fluttered down through the dark night—as the doomed Firebird let fall its glowing feathers, whose colours would never fade, though grass and leaves covered them over.

Larissa was woken by the phone. It was the duty cipher clerk, apologising for disturbing them so early—luminous clock digits showed six-thirty—but he must speak to the General Secretary urgently. Sleepily Larissa said, 'My husband's having a chat with my mother. Ring her room.' Putting the phone down, she stretched out luxuriously in the big bed.

It didn't bother her that Alexei still liked to sleep with her mother. In some ways it was quite convenient. It took the pressure off.

Westerners, she reflected, made altogether too much of sex. One's sexuality was a private matter, of small moment. If it suited her temperament to have a relationship with her father —so what? It was no one else's business.

She wasn't at all jealous of her mama. The only jealousy she felt was towards little Stiva, the son of her father's ex-mistress in Sverdlovsk. But she was learning to control even that.

Though at times she found herself making up tragedies to account for her childlessness, she wouldn't go into a decline if she never had a baby.

She had an enjoyable career, an interesting life.

Larissa stared at the darkness above her. She heard, faintly, her father speaking into the telephone. He sounded put out.

Then he was stumbling around, evidently getting dressed. She heard her mother's voice.

Larissa also could still hear some of the voices of her dream. Well, they came from the mad-house, all those poor lunatics gabbling stories to themselves, blending into a frightful chorus.

And, of course, it was being in this city, Geneva, this place of rendezvous and division, where all languages met.

Closing her eyes and turning on her side, she composed herself to sleep. Would she dream again so richly? No doubt her reading of Jung had had an effect. Perhaps she should also dip into Freud. She'd heard he had some interesting things to say about father–daughter relations. She would send someone to buy a set of his works.

She slept.

· 24 ·

The western journalists covering the summit had been having a frustrating time. Never had so many chased so much for so little. They had started off with that appalling *gaffe*, of course —assuming that Grobichov's companion was his wife. It wasn't their fault; they hadn't been properly briefed. The American information office pretended they knew all along that the lady was Grobichov's mother-in-law, but that story misled no one. They'd made a gigantic boob, and the press and media—swallowing its own small embarrassment—had been able to capitalise on it in a grand way.

If they mistook an ungainly homespun mother-in-law for a wife—or a pig for a poke, as one reporter noted for his crude wit put it—how could they be trusted to defend the interests of the West? On the other hand, Grobichov came out of the mix-up well. With one surprising, yet touching and gracious, move he had given dignity to the scorned and derided status of mother-in-law. 'Mother-in-law' became a central theme in chat-shows, and the women's interest pages of newspapers and magazines ran features on the mothers-in-law of celebrities.

The oily, pasty face of Olga Ivanovna became as famous as the faces of Grobichov himself and his beautiful young wife. Viewers and readers were constantly reminded that Grobichov had once been a humble miner, and—like miners everywhere —cherished their close-knit family lives and respected women.

How cheapjack, by comparison, was O'Reilly's entry into the summit, his attempt to steal a march on his much younger guest by appearing on the steps without an overcoat!—An attempt which, in any case, had scandalously backfired. Close analysis by speech experts revealed that the deaf-mute *Guardian* journalist was absolutely right in claiming he'd muttered, 'Fucking hell!' The pollution of Jerkoff, almost forgotten in the past few weeks, could be smelt again. Church groups revived calls for O'Reilly's impeachment.

Yet generally people were prepared to wait and see. Millions of words were spilled on the subject of how well or ill he was standing up to the pressure. Millions more, on the still more crucial question of how the summit was going. This was the prime cause of the western media's frustration—there was no news. The news black-out had held firm, with scarcely a leak. It was an affront to democracy and freedom. Journalists were reduced to guesswork and reading faces for signs.

The faces of Mako and Requiem looked gloomy, very often. It was said the first and only round table discussion had broken off in bitter acrimony; Grobichov and O'Reilly had had their 'walk in the wood' because the only alternative was to announce the break-up of the summit. Their taking the summit into their own hands was an act of desperation, and one shouldn't read hopefulness into it. Requiem, in an unguarded moment, had hinted as much. On the other hand, Mako had been heard to remark that the President and Grobichov had taken to each other; and the warm smiles and handshakes when they met seemed to bear that out.

No tangible progress in negotiations was expected, that was

clear. The question was, would they end up at least talking to each other like reasonable human beings?

The mood, as the hundreds of journalists streamed from their hotels to the International Conference Centre, on the last morning, was on the whole pessimistic. Total disaster was unlikely, if only because both leaders, for different reasons, needed to be able to fly home with their heads high. But clearly there would be no real breakthrough.

The much smaller band of East European journalists had had an excellent conference. While deploring the sordid commercialism and rank social injustices of a polluted western city, they had gorged themselves on its food and drink, and their suitcases were stuffed full with luxury goods, books and records. What had appeared a dearth of news to their western colleagues struck them as God's plenty. Spared the embarrassment of reporting Grobichov's mother-in-law as his wife, since it wasn't customary to mention family connections, they had unexpectedly been given the wink to do so—just when the beautiful and intelligent Larissa appeared on the scene! The *Tass* reporters mentioned her first, then their Warsaw Pact colleagues took up the theme. They'd all been covertly warned to drop such intimate journalism on their return home, but while in Geneva they could make hay.

Two or three of the Muscovites had even attended psychology lectures given by L. A. Grobichova, without realising they were listening to a very important politician's wife. That wasn't surprising; in the Soviet Union, a woman is judged by her own work and status, not by who her husband happens to be.

They were well aware that next week, or next month, Larissa would merge into the anonymous mass of Soviet workers, to be referred to only as L. A. Grobichova, professor in the Department of Psychology at Moscow University. That was right and proper. If she lived in a better street than most professors, and did her shopping by special Kremlin delivery, that was no one's business. Who would envy their western colleagues' hunger for sensationalism?

Yes, they were in a cheerful mood as they gathered at the International Conference Centre. Yet they, too, expected little in the way of tangible political progress. Grobichov had come, they knew, wanting a reduction of medium-range nuclear missiles in Europe. There wasn't a chance in hell that he'd get it.

· 25 ·

The digital clock showed 11.58. A tall, stooped, spectral figure walked from the wings on to the stage, and the murmurs of the assembled multitude quietened. The gaunt, aged, yet still handsome face of Stanislav Finn, Secretary General to the United Nations, gazed down at them. He spoke into the microphone a few words of welcome, then expressed, in a frail voice, his hope that the negotiations now drawing to their conclusion had not been in vain. Asking them to welcome General Secretary Grobichov and President O'Reilly, he bowed his head slightly and retired to a chair at the corner of the stage. The journalists clapped him warmly; the indomitable old battler for peace was universally respected.

An expectant hush followed. Then, dramatically, the President and the General Secretary appeared from opposite wings, marched towards each other and shook hands fervently by the microphone. The applause broke out afresh; cameras flashed. The brilliant, bulging eyes of Grobichov, gazing up, were only inches from O'Reilly's beaming, amiable smile. Their hands continued to pump. Then Grobichov withdrew to a chair. The

President produced a piece of paper and reading glasses from his breast pocket. Dominated by flags of the United States and the Soviet Union, he addressed the journalists.

'General Secretary Finn, thank you for your warm welcome. Wanda and I would also like to thank the people of Switzerland for making our stay a very pleasant one.

'Well, it's been pleasant but, gee! it's been mighty tough! Mr Grobichov and I have had some useful discussions. We found we could talk to each other. Some people didn't think we could do that. Well, we've proved them wrong. Huge differences remain between us. He didn't pull any punches, and I didn't pull any either. We didn't come here expecting we could solve any of our differences and we haven't done. If you're looking for agreements you won't find any. But what we've done is set up a dialogue. We're going to meet again. Wanda and I have invited Mr Grobichov and his lovely wife Lara to the United States, and they've invited us back. We also hope some time or other to work together in space. In the words of Tchaikovsky, we can see our future in the stars.

'I leave Geneva today full of hope and determination to build a world safe for our children to live in. General Secretary Grobichov, I ask you to join us in it. Thank you.'

O'Reilly took off his glasses and headed for a chair. The audience clapped. Finn, whose dark suit seemed over-large for his shrinking frame, slapped his bony hands together. Grobichov rose to his feet and came forward. The clapping stilled. As he began to speak, most of his audience was taken aback by the flow of almost-perfect English. He had begun the summit knowing no English. He had, several journalists would report later, speed-learnt the language in a single night.

'General Secretary Finn, I too would like to endorse the President's thanks to the people of Switzerland. They have created excellent conditions for us to work in.

'And we've done a huge amount of work, we've covered a

lot of ground. We've gone into the problems facing us in depth, and we've done it totally openly and frankly. Our talks have been very very useful. We haven't achieved everything we hoped to. The problems of peace, and in particular the need to reduce tension by withdrawing nuclear armaments from Europe, have proved too difficult, there are too many differences between us, to solve in two days . . .'

Finn lifted his hands as if to clap, but merely folded them.

'But we are going to meet again; and we in the Soviet Union are determined to do all in our power to achieve practical results. And we would very much hope that we could have the same approach from the Administration of the United States of America. Thank you for your attention.'

He turned away, removing his reading glasses. O'Reilly stood up, clapping. The two men met and pumped hands, smiling broadly. The conference centre erupted in loud applause. This was beyond anyone's expectations! Their words, and even more their tones, had been friendly; they were going to meet again; they were shaking hands and smiling like old buddies! Already the pressmen at the rear were fighting to get out and reach a telephone.

His face carefully turned away from the cameras, the President was saying: 'I bet that's put the shit up some of our hardliners!'

'You're right, Mr President!'

O'Reilly added wistfully: 'But I kind of wish we'd got an agreement on Fedora's vision. I liked that idea. In fact I still don't understand what the problem was.'

Grobichov smiled sardonically. 'Don't play games with me, Mr President. You almost had me fooled!'

They broke off to shake hands with Finn as the old diplomat was stalking off-stage. Then Grobichov said, 'Let's head for the champagne, shall we?' He lifted his arm to steer the President in Finn's wake.

'I wish Mako had woken me,' complained the President as they strolled along a corridor. 'Maybe you and I could have rescued the agreement. You said you found a mistake in our guy's translation—but did you have to tear the whole thing up? The guy was tired. It was a genuine mistake.'

'Of course I know that! I simply had an early morning call from Moscow which gave me an unpleasant shock. I began to smell the rat last night, and set a few enquiries afoot. And I found out a couple of things which you hoped I wouldn't discover till it was too late . . . I think you can guess what they are . . .' He kept his arm round O'Reilly's shoulder, and his eyes glinted amiably—even admiringly. 'First of all, that my old friend Leonid, in the last couple of years of his life, asked Saltikov-Shchedrin to re-organise our chemical warfare defences . . . We both know what that means—at this moment you could no doubt wipe out our armies without a shot being fired! No wonder you wanted us to get rid of our SS-20s!'

'I haven't been playing games.'

Grobichov, chuckling, slapped O'Reilly on the shoulder. 'We two are well matched,' he continued. 'I bear you no ill will—I'd have done the same myself. And the second thing I found out was about your plague in California. People are dying there like flies—you needn't try to deny it. I hear it's sexually transmitted, and so—*yazvitel'na*—I don't know the word—poisonous?—the whole state will soon be uninhabitable. Well, I'm sorry for California, but we don't intend to take over your plague!' He roared with laughter.

O'Reilly frowned, and said he knew nothing about chemicals.

'Oh, really? Nor about viruses? You thought you were going to sell us thirty million normal, uncontaminated contraceptives?—But that really was hitting below the belt, in more ways than one, Mr President! Not even Stalin would have dreamed that idea up!'

They reached an open door, guarded by two security men. Waiters could be seen distributing glasses of champagne, to a polite hum of American and Russian voices.

'So you won't be coming to our Olympics?'

'Don't kid me: there won't *be* any Olympics. After you, my friend.'

· 26 ·

They entered a room already crowded with back-stage workers from the rival camps, selected journalists, and negotiators. Everyone stopped, in mid-sentence or mid-swallow, to clap and cheer their leaders. There was genuine relief and euphoria in the greeting—at least on the part of those who had had to work and wait in ignorance. Their happy faces, American and Russian, seemed to be saying, 'At last, a fresh start between us!'

Grobichov walked immediately to his wife and mother-in-law. It was noted that, most courteously, he embraced the latter before kissing Larissa. The stout homely lady was in her rumpled grey overcoat and headscarf, as if she couldn't wait to get on the plane. Larissa, in sweater, skirt and flat shoes, certainly lost out in the fashion stakes, on this occasion, to Wanda in her red pants-suit, frilly white blouse, and gold high-heels. The First Lady scurried to the Tiger and gave him a warm hug. Flushed with pleasure, he noticed that even people who had given him a hard time, like Hank Klondyke of NBC, looked friendly and appreciative. Klondyke, in fact, stepped up and said, 'Congratulations, Mr President! You've done a wonderful job. I hear you toughed it out with him!'

'It's good to see you, Hank.'

'I'd say all your domestic problems are over.'

Mako, smiling, glided up. 'I'd say you're dead right there, Hank!'

'Thanks, Hank,' said O'Reilly. The veteran communicator stepped back, and turned away to replenish his glass. Mako, his arm round the President, said softly, 'It will be interesting to see what "Birch" makes of their reactions in the Kremlin, Mr President.'

'Grobichov made some pretty funny comments, Walter.'

'He was keeping his cards hidden. But we'll find out from "Birch" what he really makes of it.'

O'Reilly frowned. ' "Birch" is dead. You know that. Saltok-Chadrin was shot.'

Mako frowned. 'But he wasn't "Birch". Did you really think he was? I just thought you were pulling their legs, the other afternoon.' Staring into Tiger's puzzled eyes, Mako recalled the CIA chief's briefing; he'd spoken of Shchedrin as the likely successor to Brezhenko, before revealing 'Birch's' identity. Tiger, in the midst of all his troubles, must have misheard. A waiter stepped up to them at that moment with a tray of drinks; a couple of juniors seized the President's hands, babbling congratulations, and Mako was soon swept away in the milling throng. The President craned his neck, seeking Larissa. He saw her in a corner conversing with some reporters, and edged towards her; but people kept barring his way, eager to shake his hand and touch him, so that they could tell their grandchildren they had once touched the American President.

Larissa was relating to the present author, commissioned by *Cosmopolitan* magazine to cover the summit, her vivid, cosmopolitan dream of the night. He promised her it would be off the record.

Wanda meanwhile had trapped Grobichov against the wall; her long red fingernails were stroking his lapel and she was saying softly, 'I wanted to reassure you I'm not annoyed over what happened the other night.'

'I'm glad,' he said.

'I know you were feeling very tensed-up, just like Tiger. You've both worked very hard and done a terrific job. I thought what you said just now was perfect, Alexei. I like you a lot. Larissa's a very lucky girl.'

'*Spasibo*! Now if you'll forgive me I really ought to say thank you to—'

'—Tell me what you'll be doing when you get back to Moscow? Will you have to address the Politburo . . . ?'

'*Da, koniechno*. Of course.'

Larissa came sliding up to him, and he grabbed her hand in gratitude. O'Reilly, who had almost reached her, cursed and changed direction. 'So here we are again,' said Grobichov; 'the four of us! I shall remember our two nights together, my friends.'

'What is life,' Larissa asked languidly, 'when all is said and done, but one or two nights?'

'*Kto skazal eto*?'

'Pushkin.'

Gazing through a window at the cloudy pinnacle of Mont Blanc, O'Reilly murmured, 'It would be kind of nice if we could take a cable car up to the summit, find a little inn, and drink wine tonight in front of a roaring fire—don't you think?'

Wanda sighed. 'It would be heaven!'

'Instead of that, I'll have to address those cunts in Washington,' the Tiger growled.

'Tiger!' Wanda reprimanded with a shocked little laugh.

'Cunts?' enquired Grobichov, frowning.

'It's a very vulgar word, Alexei! It's not one you should know.'

'Vaginas,' explained Larissa coolly.

'Ah.'

He became aware of a hulking shadow. It was the burly Bogdanovich, who excused himself, in Russian, for intruding.

'You're a cunt, Bogdanovich,' growled Grobichov.

'*Shto?*'

'*Nichevo.*'

'*Vam nuzhno govorit' s'Finnom.*'

Grobichov nodded. 'Excuse me,' he said, 'I have to speak with Mr Finn for a moment.'

He disappeared in the crowd, following Bogdanovich. 'Russian is such a musical language,' murmured Wanda. 'Would you teach me a few words, Larissa, when we meet again?'

'Of course; it would be a pleasure.'

'I'd love that! Thank you! Tiger learnt a few words, didn't you? Have you found it was a help?'

The old leader didn't answer. After a few moments of silence, Wanda excused herself, saying champagne always went straight to her bladder.

'Thank God! We're alone at last!' murmured O'Reilly, swaying tiredly over her, his elbow resting on the wall. 'Larissa, I've fallen in love with you. I wanted so much to tell you this last night, when Alec and Wanda dozed off, but then I blew it by dozing off too . . . I love you. Believe me. I have to see you again . . .'

A junior aide was tugging his sleeve. O'Reilly whirled with a snarl.

'Mr President, the tarantula should be landing about now.'

'*Beat it!*'

The terrified aide backed away and vanished. O'Reilly's red exhausted eyes peered down again at Larissa. Her pure blue eyes evaded him. 'I must see you again,' he insisted.

'We're coming to visit you in June,' she murmured.

'Can we meet somewhere, alone?'

'It's impossible, in our position.'

'Oh, I thought we were coming to *you* in June. I must have got it wrong. But that's months away, Larissa. I'm old. I hear time's winged chariots of fire. June is too far away . . .'

He heard the thin, shrill voice of Requiem greeting him. He cursed again, and swung round, releasing Larissa. He couldn't tell Requiem to beat it. 'Hi, Henry,' he growled.

Requiem too was swaying a little. He held a champagne glass. Normally he drank only fruit juice, but today he had something to celebrate. He and Mako had been on the phone to Washington all night. It was becoming established that the domestic pressures against IUD could be handled—paid off, for the most part, by large contracts. There'd be no need to get the nominal collaboration of the Reds. He and Mako had been poring desperately over the agreement, trying to find some loophole, when the Reds had phoned and solved their problem. Requiem had prayed in his room for a whole hour after that, thanking God. He moved in a mysterious way.

'I drink your health, Mr President,' he slurred, lifting his glass to within inches of his flashing spectacles. A watchful security-guard, stepping back at that moment to observe a suspicious shadow outside the window, bumped Requiem in the back and dashed his champagne over the President's shirt.

'For Chrissake, Henry, watch what you're doing!' O'Reilly growled.

'I'm sorry, sir.'

Fumbling for his handkerchief, O'Reilly found instead a magazine. He remembered, and brought it out. 'I promised you this,' he said to Larissa. 'The latest *Digest*. You remember —the article on Bergman?'

She thanked him, and put the magazine in her handbag. Requiem diligently wiped O'Reilly's shirt front with his handkerchief.

Grobichov came back. O'Reilly threw one arm round his neck, the other round Larissa's. 'You're a lucky guy, Alec,' he mumbled drunkenly. 'A fucking lucky guy!'

'But so are you.'

'You know what, Alec? We should set up a joint headquarters here in Geneva, and live here most of the time, working on that Fed—that space project. And all'—he hiccuped—'live together in one house.'

Grobichov sighed humorously. Yes, it was a shame the agreement fell through. Larissa gently slid from the old man's embrace, and O'Reilly grabbed Requiem. 'That space venture, Henry! It's a damn shame we couldn't have worked together on that!'

'Well, they had their chance,' Requiem slurred. 'We'll just work on it on our own.'

Grobichov smiled. 'You think you can do it?'

'There's no question. Within ten years.'

'And how are you going to do it?' laughed Grobichov.

'With laser beams.'

'Laser beams! Well, I guess that's an improvement on old Fedorov's electricity?'

'Who's Fedorov?' asked Requiem.

'Oh, he was one of our Russian mystics. He had great visions. Larissa there—she doesn't believe it can be done—do you, darling . . . ? But I wish you luck! You think these laser beams can do the trick?'

The Russian leader's ironic chuckle infuriated Requiem. 'I'm damn sure they can,' he snarled. 'So, more important, do our scientists. Some of the greatest scientists in the world. Nobel Prize Winners. You'll be laughing on the other side of your face.'

'Really? You think you can get everyone?' chuckled Grobichov. 'Even if they lie buried under the sea!'

'Every one. Or at least ninety per cent.'

Larissa, leaning back against the wall, staring into space, murmured some lines of Pushkin:

> 'Only I, the mysterious singer,
> Cast ashore by the storm,
> Still sing my former hymns, and dry
> My wet clothes in the sun, beneath a rock . . .'

But the three men took no notice.

'Oh, ninety per cent!' laughed Grobichov. 'What a shame about the other ten per cent! That wouldn't have satisfied Fedorov!'

'It will be enough,' growled Requiem, seeing in a vision the hosts of angels and archangels descending on the day of wrath. *And when he had opened the seventh seal, there was silence in heaven* . . .

'More than enough!' chuckled the Russian.

A waiter glided up, bearing more champagne. O'Reilly released his two companions, mumbling, 'Let's drink a toast to Fedorov's vision! Where did I put my glass? Never mind, I'll have another. Fill your glasses!' The champagne chugged. 'To the resurrection of the dead!' O'Reilly intoned. 'And who was it? Tchaikovsky?'

'Tsiolkovsky,' corrected Larissa.

'Whoever he was, and whatever he believed . . .'

'That one day we shall seed the whole universe with human life,' said Larissa.

She glanced up involuntarily, and saw all creation in the shape and glowing colours of the Firebird.

Coming down to earth, she touched Requiem's arm. 'I wanted to apologise, Mr Requiem,' she said, 'for embarrassing you yesterday. At the school. It was an unfortunate misunderstanding.'

Above the babble of voices in the room, the music of Stravinsky's *Firebird Suite* soared brazenly. Larissa said to the Defence Secretary: 'That's what you should call your space research—the Firebird.'

He frowned. 'What's that?'

She explained to him the mythic bird's magic feathers; how she was seized by a black hawk and whirled into the air; how she saved the world, at the cost of her own life, by shedding her plumage, letting it rain on the earth. 'Don't you think it would be a good name, Mr Requiem?'

'I sure do!' exclaimed Requiem. 'It's meaningful and it's catchy. The Firebird . . . I think that's a great idea.' He clutched the arm of Mako, who was standing behind him with the interpreter he'd been screwing. 'Walter,' he said, 'how do you like this? The Firebird! For our lasers . . . Don't you think it sounds better than IUD?'

'You're right. It would avoid any confusion. Firebird . . . Yes, I like it . . .'

While Grobichov was being collared by Kirillov, O'Reilly took the opportunity to waylay Larissa. 'Just a few moments alone with you,' he begged.

'*Nevozmozhno*. It's impossible.'

'Just one quiet, tender kiss . . .' His thick lips lunged down; she turned her head to avoid them.

An officer of the KGB had replaced the *Firebird* with a lively, tuneful section of the *Marriage of Figaro*. The celebrants became affected by the music; so affected that, unconsciously, they began to converse in quasi-musical tones, even repeating themselves in an operatic way, not unlike the cantata for many voices rising above the confusion of Russian and English . . .

INTERPRETER: I've been listening to Kirillov, I've been listening to Kirillov . . .

MAKO: You've been listening to Kirillov . . .

INTERPRETER: What he said, I found disturbing.

MAKO: Why disturbing, why disturbing?

INTERPRETER: Well he said the IUD, IUD, IUD's extremely dangerous.

MAKO: There's no danger, there's no danger, I can guarantee its safety.

INTERPRETER: That's a blessing! I was bothered! That's a blessing! I was bothered! I was bothered, that's a blessing . . . !

O'REILLY: Just one tender, quiet moment . . .

LARISSA: *Nevozmozhno, nevozmozhno.*

WANDA (*to Grobichov*): We will stroll by the Pacific, at our beach-house by the ocean, by the ocean near LA . . .

GROBICHOV: *Nevozmozhno, nevozmozhno,* no, no, no!

WANDA: Oh, I understand your feelings, we would stroll as friends together, in the warmth of California, California, we will stroll as friends together . . .

O'REILLY: I would be your slave for ever . . .

LARISSA: *Nevozmozhno!*

GROBICHOV: *Nevozmozhno* . . . ! Ah, Kirillov, you're not drinking! Would you like another vodka?

LARISSA: I enjoyed our talk together, in that room by Lake Geneva. It was pleasant, but too dangerous . . .

O'REILLY: One tender, quiet . . .

LARISSA: *Nevozmozhno.*

O'REILLY: Ah, Larissa!